THE
LAW OF LOVE

ALSO BY LAURA ESQUIVEL

Like Water for Chocolate

THE
LAW OF LOVE

LAURA ESQUIVEL

Translated by Margaret Sayers Peden

CROWN PUBLISHERS, INC.
NEW YORK

Grateful acknowledgment is made to the following for permission to reprint previously published material:

EMI Music Publishing: Lyrics to "Burundanga" by Rafael Oscar M. Bouffartique. Copyright © 1953 renewed 1981 Morro Music Corp. All rights controlled and administered by EMI Catalogue Partnership, Inc. All rights reserved. International copyright secured. Used by permission.

Liliana Felipe: Lyrics from "Mala," "A Nadie," "San Miguel Arcángel," and "A Su Merced" by Liliana Felipe are reprinted by permission of Liliana Felipe/Ediciones El Hábito.

Universidad Nacional Autónoma de México: Poems from *Trece Poetas del Mundo Azteca* by Miguel León-Portilla are reprinted by permission of the publisher. Copyright © Secretaría de Educación Pública. All rights reserved.

Translation copyright © 1996 by Laura Esquivel
Illustrations copyright © 1995 by Miguelanxo Prado

Published by Crown Publishers, Inc., 201 East 50th Street, New York, New York 10022. Member of the Crown Publishing Group.

Random House, Inc. New York, Toronto, London, Sydney, Auckland
http://www.randomhouse.com/

CROWN is a trademark of Crown Publishers, Inc.

Originally published in Spanish by Editorial Grijalbo, S.A. de C.V., in 1995
Copyright © 1995 by Laura Esquivel

Printed in the United States of America

Design by Lauren Dong

Library of Congress Cataloging-in-Publication Data
Esquivel, Laura, 1950–
[Ley del amor. English]
The law of love / by Laura Esquivel ; translated by Margaret Sayers Peden.
I. Peden, Margaret Sayers. II. Title.
PQ7298.15.S638L4913 1996
863—dc20   96-22952

ISBN: 0-517-70681-4

10 9 8 7 6 5 4 3 2 1

First American Edition

For Sandra

For Javier

THE
LAW OF LOVE

1

I am drunk, crying, filled with grief,
Thinking, speaking,
And this I find inside:
May I never die,
May I never disappear.
There, where there is no death,
There, where death is conquered,
Let it be there that I go.
May I never die,
May I never disappear.

Ms. "Cantares mexicanos," fol. 17 v.
NEZAHUALCÓYOTL
Trece Poetas del Mundo Azteca
MIGUEL LEÓN-PORTILLA

When do the dead die? When they are forgotten. When does a city disappear? When it no longer exists in the memory of those who lived there. And when does love cease? When one begins to love anew. Of this there is no doubt.

That is why Hernán Cortés decided to construct a new city upon the ruins of the ancient Tenochtitlán. The time it took him to size up the situation was the same that it takes a firmly gripped sword to pierce the skin of the chest and reach the center of the heart: one second. But in time of battle, a split second can mean escaping the sword or being run through by it.

During the conquest of Mexico, only those who could react in an instant survived, those who so feared death that they placed all their instincts, all their reflexes, all their senses, at the service of that fear. Terror became the command center for all their actions. Located just behind the navel, it received before the brain all the sensations perceived by smell, sight, touch, hearing, and taste. These were processed in milliseconds and forwarded to the brain, along with a precise course of action. All this lasted no more than the one second essential for survival.

As rapidly as the Conquistadors' bodies were acquiring the ability to react, new senses were also evolving. They learned to anticipate an attack from the rear, smell blood before it was spilled, sense a betrayal before the first word was uttered, and, above all, to see into the future as well as the keenest oracle. This was why, on the very day Cortés saw an Indian sounding a conch in front of the remains of an ancient pyramid, he knew he could not leave the city in ruins. It would have been like leaving a monument to the grandeur of the Aztecs. Sooner or later, nostalgia would have prompted the Indians to regroup in an attempt to regain their city. There was no time to lose. He had to obliterate all trace of the great Tenochtitlán from Aztec memory. He had to construct a new city before it was too late.

What Cortés did not take into account was that stones contain a truth beyond what the eye manages to see. They possess a force of their own that is not seen but felt, a force that cannot be constrained by a house or church. None of Cortés's newly acquired senses was fine-tuned enough to perceive this force. It was too subtle. Invisibility granted it absolute mobility, allowing it to swirl silently about the heights of the pyramids without being noticed. Some were aware of its effects, but didn't know what to attribute them to. The most severe case was that of Rodrigo Díaz, one of Cortés's valiant captains. As he and his companions proceeded to demolish the pyramids, he could never have imagined the consequences of his fateful contact with the stones. Even if someone had warned Rodrigo that those stones were powerful enough to change his life, he would not have believed it, for his beliefs never went beyond what he could grasp with his hands. When he was told there was one pyramid where the Indians used to conduct pagan ceremonies honoring some sort of goddess of love, he laughed. Not for a moment did he allow that any such goddess could exist, let alone that the pyramid could have a sacred function. Everyone agreed with him; they decided it was not even worth bothering to erect a church there. Without further thought, Cortés offered Rodrigo the site where the pyramid stood, so that he could build his house upon it.

Rodrigo was a happy man. He had earned the right to this parcel of land by his achievements on the battlefield and by his fierceness in hacking off arms, noses, ears, and heads. By his own hand he had dispatched approximately two hundred Indians, so he did not have to wait long for his reward: a generous tract of land bordering one of the four canals running through the city, the one that in time would become the road to Tacuba. Rodrigo's ambition made him dream of erecting his house in a grander spot— even on the ruins of the Great Temple—but he was forced to content himself with this more modest site since there were already plans to build a cathedral where that temple once stood. However, as compensation for his plot not being located within the select circle of houses the captains were building in the center of the city as witness to the birth of New Spain, he was granted an *encomienda*; that is, along with the land, ownership of fifty Indians, among whom was Citlali.

Citlali was descended from a noble family of Tenochtitlán. From childhood she had received a privileged upbringing, so her bearing reflected no trace of submission but, rather, great pride verging on defiance. The graceful swaying of her broad hips charged the atmosphere with sensuality, spreading ripples of air in widening circles. This energy displacement was much like the waves generated when a stone is dropped suddenly into a calm lake.

Rodrigo sensed Citlali's approach at a hundred yards. He had survived the Conquest for good reason: he possessed an acute ability to detect movements outside the ordinary. Interrupting his activity, he tried to pinpoint the danger. From the heights of the pyramid he commanded a view of everything in its vicinity. Immediately he focused on the line of Indians approaching his property. In the lead came Citlali. Rodrigo instantly realized that the movement that had so disturbed him emanated from Citlali's hips. He was completely disarmed. This was a challenge he did not know how to confront, and so he fell captive to the spell of her hips. All this happened as his hands were engaged in the effort of moving the stone that had formed the apex of the Pyramid of Love. But before he could do so there was a moment for the powerful energy generated by the pyramid to circulate through his veins. It was a lightning current, a blinding flash that made him see Citlali not as the simple Indian servant that she appeared to be, but rather, as the Goddess of Love herself.

Never had Rodrigo desired anyone so greatly, much less an Indian woman. He could not have explained what came over him. He hurriedly finished dislodging the stone and awaited her arrival. As soon as she drew near him, he could no longer restrain himself; he ordered all the other Indians off to install themselves at the rear of the property and right there, in the heart of what had once been the temple, he raped her.

Citlali, her face motionless and her eyes wide open, regarded her image reflected in Rodrigo's green eyes. Green, green, the color of the sea that she had seen once as a child. The sea which still brought fear to her. Long ago she had sensed the enormous destructive power latent in each wave. From the moment she had learned that the white-skinned men would come from beyond the boundless waters, she had lived in terror. If they possessed the power to dominate the sea, surely it meant that they carried inside them an equal capacity for destruction. And she had not been mistaken. The sea had arrived to destroy all of her world. She felt its furious pounding inside her. Not even the weight of the heavens above Rodrigo's shoulders could halt the frenzied movement of that sea. Deep within her its salty waves burned like fire, and its battering made her dizzy and nauseous. Rodrigo entered her body the same way he made his way through life: with the luxury of violence.

He had arrived some time earlier, during one of the battles that preceded the fall of the great Tenochtitlán, on the very day that Citlali had given birth to her son. As a result of her noble lineage, Citlali had been closely attended despite the fierce battle her people were waging against the Spanish. Her son had arrived in this world to the sounds of defeat, to the groans of a dying Tenochtitlán. The midwife who attended her, trying somehow to compensate for the child's untimely arrival, begged the Gods to provide him with good fortune. The Gods must have foreseen that the child's best fate lay not on this earth, for when the midwife handed the baby to Citlali to embrace, the mother held him in her arms for the first and last time. Just then Rodrigo, having killed the guards of the royal palace, burst in on her, wrested the newborn from her hands, and dashed him to the ground. Seizing Citlali by the hair, he dragged her a short distance away and stabbed her. He cut off the arm the midwife raised against him, and as a final gesture, set fire to the palace.

O that we might decide at what moment to die. Citlali would have chosen to die that very day, the day her husband, her son, her home, her city, all died. O that her eyes had never witnessed the great Tenochtitlán robed in desolation. O that her ears had never rung with the silence of the conches. O that the earth she walked upon had not responded with the dull echoes of sand. O that the air had not been heavy with the odor of olives. O that her body had never felt another so loathsome inside itself, and O that Rodrigo in leaving had taken with him the smell of the sea.

And now, as Rodrigo rose and was adjusting his clothing, Citlali begged the Gods for the strength to live until the day that this man should repent for having profaned not only her, but the Goddess of Love. For he could not have committed a greater outrage than to violate her on such a sacred site. Citlali was sure that the Goddess must be greatly offended. The force she had felt circulating inside her, urged on by Rodrigo's savage appetite, in no way resembled the energy of love. It was a brutal force she had never known before. Once, when the pyramid was still standing, Citlali had participated in a ceremony on its heights that had produced an entirely different effect. Perhaps this difference stemmed from the fact that the pyramid was now truncated and lacked its highest point, so that amorous energy swirled about madly without any order. Poor Goddess of Love! Surely she felt as humiliated and profaned as her devoted follower Citlali, and surely she not only authorized, but eagerly awaited, the hour of their revenge.

Citlali decided that the best means of accomplishing this was to vent her rage upon someone Rodrigo loved. That was why she was delighted to learn one day that a Spanish lady would soon be arriving to wed Rodrigo. Citlali surmised that if Rodrigo was planning to marry, it must be because he was in love. She did not know that he was doing so only to fulfill one of the requirements of the *encomienda*. This specified that to combat idolatry the *encomendero* was obliged to begin constructing a church on his lands within six months from the date of receiving the royal grant; he was also to erect and inhabit a residence within eighteen months, and to transport his wife there or marry within the same period. Therefore, as soon as construction was sufficiently advanced for the house to be occupied, Rodrigo sent to Spain for Doña Isabel de Góngora, to make her his wife. The marriage took place immediately, and Citlali was placed in the lady's service as a maid in waiting. Their first encounter was neither agreeable nor disagreeable. It simply never occurred.

For a meeting to take place, two people must come together in the same space, but neither of these women inhabited the same house. Isabel continued to live in Spain, Citlali in Tenochtitlán. They had no way of ever meeting, much less communicating, for they did not speak the same language. Neither of them could recognize herself in the eyes of the other. Neither of the two shared a common landscape. Neither of the two could understand what the other said. And this was not a matter of comprehension, it was a matter of the heart, for that is where words acquire their true meaning. And the hearts of both were closed.

To Isabel, Tlatelolco was a filthy place swarming with Indians, where she was forced to go for supplies and where it was nearly impossible to find saffron or olive oil. For Citlali, Tlatelolco was the place she had most loved to visit as a child, not only because there she could savor a wealth of smells, colors, and sounds, but because there she could witness a marvelous spectacle: a man all the children called Teo, but whose real name was Teocuicani or "Divine Singer," would dance small gods on the palm of his hand. These clay gods he had shaped would speak, wage war, and sing in the voices of conches, rattles, birds, rain, thunder, all of which poured forth from the prodigious vocal cords of this man. Citlali could not hear the word "Tlatelolco" without those images springing to mind, just as the sound of the word "Spain" threw a shroud of indifference over her soul.

For Isabel it was just the opposite: Spain was the most beautiful place she knew; Spain, the richest in meaning. It was the grass of the plains, where countless times she had lain observing the sky; it was the winds off the sea that chased the clouds till they scattered across the mountain peaks. It was laughter, music, wine, wild horses, bread hot from the oven, sheets spread out in the sun to dry, the solitude of the plain, its silence. And within this solitude and this silence, made even deeper by the sound of the waves and of cicadas, Isabel had a thousand times imagined her ideal love. Spain meant the sun, heat, and love. For Citlali, Spain was the place where Rodrigo had learned how to kill.

This great difference in associations stemmed from their great difference in experience. Isabel would have to have lived a long time in Tenochtitlán to know what it meant to say *ahuehuetl*, to know how, after participating in a ceremony in its honor, one felt to rest beneath its shade. Citlali would have to have been born in Spain to know how it felt to sit among olive trees gazing at flocks of sheep. Isabel would have to have grown up with a tortilla in her hand not to be offended by its dank smell. Citlali would have to have been suckled in a place filled with the aroma of fresh-baked bread in order to delight in its taste. And both women would have to have been born with less arrogance to be able to set aside all that separated them and to discover the many things they had in common.

They walked on the same paths, were warmed by the same sun, were awakened by the same birds, were caressed by the same hands and kissed by the same lips; yet they found not a single point of contact, not even in Rodrigo. While Isabel saw in Rodrigo the man she had dreamed of long ago in Spain, Citlali saw only her son's murderer. Neither of the two saw him as he really was, for Rodrigo was not easy to fathom. Two people lived inside him. He had but one tongue, yet it slipped into the mouths of Citlali and Isabel in very different ways. He had but one voice, yet its tones were like a caress to one and an assault to the other. He had but one pair of green eyes, yet for one they resembled a warm, tranquil sea; for the other, a sea that was restless and violent. This sea nonetheless generated life in the wombs of Isabel and Citlali indiscriminately. However, while Isabel awaited the arrival of her son with great joy, Citlali did so with horror. She aborted the fetus as she had done each time she became pregnant by Rodrigo. She could not stand the idea of bringing a being into the world that was half Indian, half Spanish. She did not believe it could harbor two such distinct natures and live in peace. It would be like condemning her child to live constantly at war with himself, fixing him forever at a crossroads, and that could never be called living.

Rodrigo himself knew this better than anyone. He had to divide his body into two separate Rodrigos. Each fought for control of his heart, which would completely change according to which of the sides was winning. To Isabel he behaved like a gentle breeze; but with Citlali, his unrestrained passion, stubborn desire, scorching lust, all caused him to act like a male in rut. He pursued her constantly; he besieged her, he lay in ambush for her, he cornered her; yet every day she seemed farther away.

During the Conquest, his sensory acuity had enabled him to survive; now it was killing him. He couldn't sleep, couldn't eat, couldn't think of anything except losing himself in Citlali's body. Now he lived only to detect the sensuous swaying of her hips in the air. No movement she made, however slight, went unnoticed by Rodrigo: he would sense it immediately, and a searing urgency would impel him to become one with its source, to unburden himself between those legs, to fall down with Citlali no matter where, to mount her day and night, trying to find relief. No day went by that he did not accost her repeatedly. His body needed a rest. He could not take any more. Not even at night could he find respite, for the moment she turned over on her straw mat, the movement of her hips created waves that swept over him with the force of a powerful groundswell. He would rise from his bed and rush like an arrow straight for Citlali.

Rodrigo thought there was no better way to show his love for Citlali; yet, Citlali never took it that way. She suffered his assaults with great stoicism, but never responded to his passion. Her soul remained unknown to him. Only once did she attempt to communicate something to him, to ask him a favor; unfortunately, on that one occasion Rodrigo could do nothing to satisfy her wish.

That evening Citlali had been watering the flowers along the balconies when she spotted a group of people dragging along a madman whose hands had been cut off. Her heart froze when she saw it was Teo, who had made the clay gods dance on his hands in the market of Tlatelolco when she was a girl. Driven mad during the Conquest, he had been discovered wandering about, singing and dancing his clay gods before crowds of children. Now he was being brought before the Viceroy, who was dining at Rodrigo's home, so that his fate could be determined. They had already cut off his hands to make sure he would never again disobey the royal edict forbidding clay idols. As soon as the Viceroy heard the case, he determined they must also cut out this madman's tongue, for he was known to incite rebellion with his stirring words in Nahuatl.

With her eyes Citlali begged Rodrigo to be merciful with Teo, but Rodrigo was caught between the sword and the wall. The Viceroy had come to visit him because there had been alarming reports that Rodrigo was becoming too lenient with the Indians of his *encomienda*; his neighbors had also witnessed him treating Citlali with uncommon indulgence. The Viceroy had subtly threatened to strip Rodrigo of his Indians, along with the other honors and privileges he had won during the Conquest. So now Rodrigo could not speak in favor of the Indian, because by doing so he would risk being accused of encouraging idolatry among the natives, an offense severe enough to retract the *encomienda*, and the last thing Rodrigo wanted to risk was losing Citlali. So he lowered his gaze and pretended not to have seen the entreaty in her eyes.

Citlali never forgave him for this. She spoke not another word to him for the rest of her life, and shut herself off forever inside her own world.

And so the house was left inhabited by beings who never communicated with one another. They were beings incapable of seeing each other, hearing each other, loving each other; they were beings who rejected each other in the belief that they belonged to very different cultures. They never discovered the true reason for this rejection. It remained unseen, issuing from the subterranean forces of the stones that had formed the Temple of Love and those of the house later built upon it: from the vexation of the pyramid, which was only awaiting the proper moment to shake off those alien stones and thereby regain its equilibrium.

Citlali's plight was similar to that of the pyramids, with the exception that, for her, regaining her former equilibrium meant not shaking off stones but seeking a means of revenge. Fortunately for her, she did not have long to wait. Isabel gave birth to a beautiful golden-haired boy. Citlali never left her side during the delivery, and as soon as the baby was delivered into the midwife's hands, Citlali took it in her arms to present to Rodrigo; then, pretending to trip, she let the child fall. He died instantly, and as he fell to the ground Citlali's lifelines fell from her hands with him.

Her time on earth was now marked in the air, among Isabel's wails and laments; it no longer belonged to her. In the confusion of the moment, Rodrigo dragged Citlali from the room by her hair, thus removing her from the scene before anyone else had time to react. He could not allow someone else's hand to harm her. Only he himself could give her a worthy death. There was no escape for Citlali, that much he knew; but he also realized that this body he had so often held, this body that he knew so well, that he had longed for and kissed so many times, merited a loving death. With great sorrow Rodrigo drew his dagger and, just as he had seen the Aztec priests do during human sacrifices, he split open Citlali's chest and took her heart in his hand, kissing it repeatedly before finally ripping it out and hurling it far away. It happened so quickly that Citlali did not experience the least suffering. Her face reflected great tranquillity and her soul at last could rest in peace, for she had wrought her revenge. But what she never realized was that her revenge lay not in having murdered the infant but in having committed an act warranting death. For it was by her own death that she finally achieved what she had so longed for after that first encounter with Rodrigo: that he be made to howl in pain.

Isabel died at almost the same time as Citlali, convinced that Rodrigo had gone mad at the sight of his dead son and so had brutally murdered Citlali. That is what was whispered in her ear; that was all they told her. For there was no need to tell a dying woman that immediately after her husband had killed Citlali, he had killed himself.

Can it be that this earth is our only abode?
I know nothing but suffering, for only in anguish
    do we live.
Will my flesh be sown anew
In my father and my mother?
Will I yet take shape as an ear of corn?
Will I throb once again in fruit?
I weep: no one is here; they have been left orphans.
Is it true we still live
In that region where all are united?
Do our hearts, perhaps, believe it so?

Ms. "Cantares mexicanos," fol. 13 v.
Nezahualcóyotl
Trece Poetas del Mundo Azteca
Miguel León-Portilla

2

*The pyramids of Parangaricutirimícuaro
are parangaricutirimicized.
He who can unparangaricutirimicute them
will be a great unparangaricutirimizator.*

There is nothing easy about being a Guardian Angel. But being Anacreonte, Azucena's Guardian Angel, is really tough, because Azucena never listens to reason. She is used to having her own blessed way, and let me tell you, in her case, "blessed" has nothing to do with divine. She simply won't recognize the existence of any will superior to her own, and so has never followed a single order except that dictated by her own desires. Using poetic license, shall we say that, for all she cares, you can take divine will and hurl it to kingdom come. To top it off, she has the royal nerve to decide that it's only fitting and just that she finally encounter her twin soul, since she has already suffered enough and isn't in the mood to wait another lifetime. With serene stubbornness she has worked her way through all the red tape necessary to convince the bureaucrats to let her make contact with Rodrigo.

I'm not criticizing her; it seemed like a good idea to me. She knows how to listen to her inner voice and, through sheer force of will, to vanquish every obstacle in her path. So she is convinced that she has triumphed because of her nerve, but that's where she's wrong. If everything works out, it will be only because her inner voice happens to be in complete accord with Divine Will, with the cosmic order in which we all have a place, a place that is ours alone. When we find it, all is in harmony; we glide smoothly along the river of life, at least until we meet an obstacle. For when even one stone is out of place, it hinders the flow of the current and the water becomes stagnant and putrid.

It's easy enough to detect disorder in the "real" world; what's difficult is to discover the hidden order in things that cannot be seen. Few have this power, and among them are artists, who are supreme Reconcilers. With their special perception they decide where on the canvas to place the yellow, blue, and red; where the notes and silences fall; what the first word of the poem should be. They go along fitting these pieces together, guided only by that inner voice telling them, "This goes here," or "That doesn't go there," until the last piece falls into place.

This predetermined ordering of colors, sounds, or words means that a work of art achieves a purpose beyond the simple satisfaction of its creator. It means that even before it is made, it has already been assigned a unique place in the human soul. So when a poet arranges the words of a poem in accordance with Divine Will, he reconciles something within each of us, for his work is in harmony with a cosmic order. As a result, his creation will flow unimpeded through our veins, creating a powerful unifying bond.

If artists are the supreme Reconcilers, there exist along with them some consummate Wreckoncilers—those who believe that theirs is the only will that matters and have power enough to *make* it matter; those who believe they have the authority to decide others' fates. Substituting lies for truth, death for life, and hatred for love inside our hearts, they repeatedly dam the flow of the river of life.

Surely the heart is not a fitting place to house hatred. But where is its place? I don't know. That is one of the universe's Unknowns. It would seem that the Gods truly delight in messing things up, for in not having created a particular spot to house hatred, they have provoked eternal chaos. Hatred is forever hunting down a refuge, poking its nose where it shouldn't, taking over sites reserved for others, invariably forcing out love.

And Nature, which, unlike the Gods, insists upon order—to the point of neurosis, you might say—feels the need to get into the act and put things back in place, thereby preserving the balance. She simply will not permit hatred to take up permanent residence in the heart, for its energy would block the circulation of love, with the grave danger that, just like stagnant water, the soul would putrefy. So instead she attempts to root out hatred whenever it settles in the heart.

This is relatively easy to do when it has made its way there by mistake or carelessness. In most of these cases all one needs to do is to be exposed to art created by a Reconciler, for in the process the soul can separate itself from the body: through the subtle alchemy of colors, sounds, forms, the soul is enabled to rise to great heights. The energy of hatred, on the other hand, is so heavy that it cannot detect subtleties, and so is unable to ascend with the soul. It remains with the body, but since its host has vacated the premises, it decides to search elsewhere for a promising spot. When the soul then returns to the body, there is room once again for love to resume its place in the heart.

The real problem arises when hatred is planted in our hearts through the conscious designs of a Wreckonciler, as when we find ourselves harmed through robbery, torture, lies, betrayal, murder. In such cases, the only way hatred can be removed is by the aggressor himself. As stipulated by the Law of Love: the person who causes an imbalance in the cosmic order is the only one who can restore balance. In nearly all cases, one lifetime is insufficient to achieve that, so Nature provides reincarnation in order to give Wreckoncilers the chance to straighten out their screwups. When hatred exists between two people, life will bring them together as many times as necessary for that hatred to disappear. Again and again they will be born near each other, until finally they learn how to love. And one day, after perhaps fourteen thousand lives, they will have learned enough about the Law of Love to be allowed to meet their twin soul. This is the highest reward a human being can ever hope for in life, and it will happen to all, you may be sure, but only at the appointed hour.

And that is precisely what my dear Azucena fails to understand. The moment finally has come for her to meet Rodrigo, but it is not yet time for them to live together side by side. First of all, she had better get some control over her emotions, and he too has some outstanding debts to pay. He has to put a few things in order before he'll be able to unite with her for all time, and Azucena is going to have to help him. Let's hope it all works out to the bene-fit of both mortals and spirits alike.

But I know how hard it will be. To succeed in her mission, Azu-cena will need a lot of help. As her Guardian Angel, I am obliged to come to her aid. And, as my protégée, she is supposed to yield and follow instructions. And that's where the tough part comes in. She doesn't heed me in the slightest. I spend five minutes explain-ing to her that she has to deactivate the protective auric field around her apartment so that Rodrigo can get in, and it's as if I were talking to the wall. She's so excited about the idea of meeting him that she has no ears for any suggestions from me. Well, we'll see if the poor guy doesn't get zapped as soon as he tries to get through that door.

But at least it won't be my fault. I've told her a thousand times what she has to do, but No Way! What worries me most is that if she isn't even capable of following such a simple order, what's going to happen when her life depends on it? In any case, may God's will be done!

3

It wasn't until her apartment alarm began to sound that Azucena realized what Anacreonte had been trying to tell her. She had completely forgotten to turn it off! This was serious, since Rodrigo's aura was not registered in the electromagnetic system protecting her apartment. If she did not deactivate the alarm immediately, the apparatus would process him as an unknown body and his cells would be prevented from correctly reintegrating inside the aerophone booth. After waiting all this time, how could she end up doing something so stupid! At best, Rodrigo would run the risk of disintegrating for twenty-four hours. She had only ten seconds to act. Fortunately, the power of love is invincible, and what the human body can accomplish in emergencies, truly amazing. In a flash, Azucena crossed the living room, deactivated the alarm, and returned to the aerophone door with time remaining to adjust her hair and put on her best smile to welcome Rodrigo.

A smile Rodrigo never saw; for as soon as his eyes fixed upon hers, the most marvelous of all encounters began: the meeting of twin souls, where physical features play a minor role. The heat from the lovers' gaze melts the barrier imposed by the flesh and allows a mutual contemplation of souls—souls that, in being identical, recognize each other's energy as their own. This recognition begins in energy receptors in the human body called chakras. There are seven chakras, each corresponding to a note on the musical scale and to a color in the rainbow. When a chakra is activated by the energy originating from the twin soul, it vibrates at its highest potential, producing a sound. In the case of twin souls, as each chakra resonates, so does that of its twin, and these two identical tones generate a subtle energy that courses through the spinal column, rising to the brain center and bursting outward to fall like a shower of color saturating the aura from top to bottom.

During their soul coupling, Azucena and Rodrigo repeated this process with each of their chakras until their auric field formed a complete rainbow and their chakras sounded a wondrous melody.

There is a vast difference between the coupling of bodies with unlike souls and the bodies of twin souls. In the former case, there is an urgency for physical possession, and, however intense the relationship becomes, it will always be conditioned by the physical. Thus a perfect communion of souls can never be achieved, however great the affinity between the two bodies. The most they can experience is great physical pleasure, but nothing more.

The case of twin souls is so intriguing because the fusion of souls is complete, occurring on all levels. Just as there is a place within a woman's body meant to be filled by the male member, so there is space between the atoms of each body free to be filled by energy from the twin soul. In this reciprocal penetration, each space becomes at the same time both contained by and containing the other: fountain and water, sword and wound, sun and moon, sea and sand, penis and vagina. The sensation of penetrating space is comparable only to that of feeling oneself penetrated; moistening, only to that of being moistened; sucking, to that of being sucked; flooded with warm sperm, only to that of ejaculating it. And when all the spaces between all the atoms in the body have filled or been filled—for the effect is the same—what follows is profound, intense, prolonged orgasm. There is nothing separating the two souls, for they form a single being. Thus restored to their original state, they are made aware of the truth: each sees, in the face of the partner, all of the faces the other has had during the fourteen thousand lives prior to their encounter.

At this moment Azucena no longer knew who was who, or what part of her body belonged to her and what to Rodrigo. She could feel a hand, but she did not know whether it was his or hers. Nor did she know who was inner and who was outer, who above and who below, who in front and who behind. All she knew was that with Rodrigo she formed a single body that, lulled by orgasms, danced through space to the rhythm of the music of the spheres.

Azucena came back to earth in her bed to find a strange leg on top of her own. She knew instantly that this leg did not belong to her: it was neither hers nor Rodrigo's. Rodrigo must have seen it too, because they screamed in unison as they discovered the body of a dead man lying between them.

The return to reality could not have been more brutal. Their honeymoon chamber was suddenly filled with policemen, reporters, and curious onlookers. Abel Zabludowsky, microphone in hand and perched on Azucena's side of the bed, was at that very moment interviewing the campaign manager of the American candidate for Planetary President, who had just been assassinated.

"Do you have any idea who might have shot Mr. Bush?"

"I haven't a clue."

"Do you believe that this assassination is part of a plot to destabilize the United States of America?"

"It's hard to tell. This cowardly assassination has definitely jolted our consciousness, and I, as well as all the inhabitants of the Planet, can only lament the fact that violence has returned to cast its dark shadow over us all. I want to take this opportunity to publicly express my total condemnation of any act of this nature, and to demand that the Planetary Prosecutor General conduct an immediate investigation into the cause of this crime, as well as the identity of those who masterminded it. Today is certainly a day of mourning for us all."

The manager of the presidential campaign, like everyone else around the world, was aghast. For more than a century, crime had been nonexistent on Planet Earth. This inexplicable act, however, presaged a return to an age of violence that everyone believed had been left behind.

It took Azucena and Rodrigo a moment to recover from their shock. Rodrigo had no idea what was going on, but Azucena did: she had forgotten to turn off the alarm clock on her Televirtual set. She groped for the remote control on her night table and shut it off. Immediately, the images of everyone at the murder scene vanished, though the bitter taste lingering in their mouths did not. Azucena felt nauseous. She was not used to confronting violence, much less in such a brutal, immediate way.

Televirtuality in effect transports the viewer to the site of news events, placing one right in the middle of the action. Strangely enough, that was why Azucena had bought her set, because it was so pleasant to wake up during the weather report. She might find herself anywhere in the world, or the galaxy, for that matter. She could revel in exotic landscapes or delight in the ordinary; open her eyes to the dawn on Saturn, or hear the sound of the Neptunian sea; luxuriate in the luminous dusk on Jupiter or in the freshness of a forest just after a downpour. There was no better way to wake up before going off to work.

She certainly had not expected such a violent jolt, especially after such a marvelous night. What a nightmare! She could not get the picture out of her mind: a man with a bullet in his head lying right in the middle of her bed. Her bed! The bed that was Rodrigo's and hers, now tainted with death. But as she gazed once again into Rodrigo's eyes, she regained her soul and her horror evaporated. And at the touch of his arms, she was again in Paradise. She would have remained there forever had Rodrigo not gotten up. He wanted to go to his apartment to collect his belongings and return to her, never to be separated again. Before he left, Azucena promised that he would find no disagreeable surprises upon his return, for she would disconnect all electronic devices in her home and leave the aerophone alarm deactivated. Rodrigo responded with a broad smile . . . and that was the last image Azucena had of him.

The first thing Azucena missed when she reawakened was a sense of well-being upon seeing the sunlight. Anguish unfolded its black wings above her, engulfing her in darkness, stifling her voice, extinguishing pleasure, freezing the sheets on her bed, silencing the music of the stars. The party was over before they had danced their tango, before she had wept with pleasure at dawn, before she could tell Rodrigo that he drove her mad with delight. She felt the words knot in her throat; she could not bear to speak them or to hear them. A large part of her being had flowed out to fill the spaces between the cells of Rodrigo's body. She had literally been emptied. And of her night of love, all that remained was a sweet pain in her intimate parts, and here and there a bruise of passion. That was all.

But these bruises faded in time, and what were once violets in the fields of ecstasy became pale witnesses to her abandonment and her loneliness. As her physical pain diminished, her internal muscles, which with such pleasure had received, squeezed, clung to, moistened, and savored Rodrigo, resumed their former state, and her body was left with no palpable memory of her brief honeymoon.

What doubt can there be that distance is one of the greatest torments for lovers? Azucena felt a profound, consuming emptiness. Losing her twin soul meant losing her very being.

Azucena knew this, and sought desperately to find Rodrigo's soul. She began by retracing his footsteps, by penetrating the spaces where he had been. This popular home remedy worked for a while, since at first Rodrigo's soul was still very much there; but as time passed, Azucena could scarcely perceive his aura, could barely remember him, his smell, his taste, his warmth. Her memory clouded over with suffering. The spaces between the cells of her body shrank back in sadness as, inevitably, Rodrigo's soul began to escape her.

Rodrigo's disappearance had left her completely disheartened, without recourse to reason. What explanation could she give to her body, which was begging to be caressed? And, above all, what was she going to tell that busybody Cuquita, her super? Azucena had rushed to her that first day to ask her to register Rodrigo's aura in the building's master control as soon as he returned, and now she felt like a fool. Every time she ran into Cuquita, the super would ask, sarcasm dripping from each word, when her twin soul would be returning. Cuquita hated her. They had never gotten along, because Cuquita was a social malcontent who belonged to the Party for the Retribution of Inequities—the PRI.

Cuquita had always spied on her, trying to catch her at something, just once, in order not to feel so inferior to Azucena. She had never succeeded, but now she had Azucena at a disadvantage, and it irritated Azucena to be the object of her ridicule. What could she tell Cuquita? She didn't know. The only one who had answers, who definitely knew Rodrigo's whereabouts, was her Guardian Angel, Anacreonte, but Azucena had broken off communication with him. She had not been interested in any information he had to offer. Now she was furious. He had known perfectly well that the only thing in life that interested her was finding Rodrigo, so why hadn't he warned her that Rodrigo might disappear? What the hell good was it to have a Guardian Angel if he couldn't prevent that kind of disaster? She would never listen to him again. That good-for-nothing would see she didn't need him to manage her life.

Her worst problem was that she didn't know where to begin. Besides, even going out of the house depressed her. In the wake of the assassination, the atmosphere was tense and everyone was afraid. If someone had dared commit murder, what next? That was it—the assassination! Why hadn't she thought of it before? What happened to Rodrigo probably had something to do with the murder. Perhaps new disturbances were preventing him from returning, and there she was, behaving like a catatonic jerk, waiting for her lover to fall out of the sky. Quickly, she switched on her Telervirtual. It had been a week since she'd paid any attention to the outside world.

Azucena's bedroom was instantly converted into a cocoa plantation that was being destroyed by army troops. The voice of Abel Zabludowsky reported: "Today the American Army struck a ferocious blow against cocoa trafficking. Several acres of the drug were destroyed, and one of the most powerful chocolate lords was captured after being sought for some time by police. No further information is available at this time. The names of the leader and his group are being withheld so as not to jeopardize the investigation, which has targeted the entire Venus cartel."

Azucena's bedroom was then transformed into a laboratory filled with computers for the ensuing documentary on how crime had been abolished from Planet Earth. This had resulted from the development of an apparatus that, from a single drop of blood or saliva, a broken fingernail or a hair, could reconstruct the entire body of a person and indicate his whereabouts. Criminals, therefore, could be arrested and punished minutes after committing an offense, no matter where they had transflashed themselves.

Predictably, however, the candidate's assassin had been very careful not to leave any traces behind. All the spit on the sidewalk had been analyzed, to no avail. There had been no sign of the criminal. Suddenly, the laboratory images vanished, to be replaced by Abel Zabludowsky and Dr. Díez. Both were sitting on Azucena's bed, one on either side of her. Azucena was shocked to see her colleague at the clinic being interviewed by Abel Zabludowsky.

"Welcome, Dr. Díez. Thank you for joining us here on our program . . ."

"My pleasure."

"Tell us, Doctor, just what is this new device you've invented?"

"Well, it's really very simple. It photographs a person's aura, and detects traces of others who have been in contact with that person.

This device makes it easy to determine who was the last person to approach Mr. Bush."

"Just a moment, I don't think I completely understand. You mean that with this apparatus you've invented, you can capture, in a single photograph of someone's aura, *all* the people who have been in contact with that person?"

"That's correct. The aura consists of energy, which we have been able to photograph for quite some time now. We all know that when a person penetrates our magnetic field, he contaminates it. We have countless aurographs recording the moment at which an aura is affected but, until now, no one has been able to analyze and determine to whom the aura of the contaminating body belonged. That is what my device can do. And if we have the aurograph of the contaminating party, we can reproduce the body of the person to whom it belongs."

"Let me get this straight. Mr. Bush was assassinated as he was making his way through a large crowd. Many people must have been close enough to have contaminated his aura. So how can we be sure which is the assassin's?"

"By its color. You recall that all negative emotions have a specific color. . . ."

Azucena did not need to hear any more. Besides being her colleague, Dr. Díez was a close friend, so all she had to do was to go see him, have her own aurograph taken, and thus be able to find Rodrigo. Thank God! She grabbed her purse and rushed out, without even putting on shoes, without combing her hair, and without turning off her Televirtual set. Had she waited just another minute, she would have seen Rodrigo leaping about her bedroom like a madman. Abel Zabludowsky had moved on to the interplanetary newscast. Korma, a penal planet, had just suffered a volcanic eruption. All Televirtualites were being asked to send aid to the victims, since the inhabitants of that planet, members of the Third World, were living in the Stone Age. Among them was Rodrigo, who was desperately trying to escape a sea of lava.

Rodrigo was the last to enter a small cave toward the top of a mountain. Even the smallest of the primitive creatures inhabiting the planet Korma could run more rapidly than he. He lacked calloused feet to protect him against sharp rocks and heat, and his muscles were not used to such physical exertion. The most he had been called on to do in his lifetime was walk to the nearest aerophone booth to be transported elsewhere on the planet. He did not remember at what moment he had entered the booth that had flashed him here. In fact, he did not remember anything at all; he only felt a sense of anguish, as if he had failed to do something vital. His body longed for something he did not know; his feet wanted to tango, his lips felt the urgent need for a kiss; his voice strained to speak a name that was erased from his memory. He was at the point of uttering it, but his mind drew a blank. The only thing he was sure of was that he missed the moon . . . and that this cave stank to high heaven.

The concentrated humors of some thirty primitive creatures— men, women, and children—were unbearable. The combined sweat, urine, excrement, semen, rotting food, blood, earwax, mucus, and other secretions accumulating for years on the bodies of these savages was powerful enough to make anyone reel. But even more powerful than the stench was Rodrigo's need to catch his breath after the marathon he had just run, so he gulped in great mouthfuls of air and then collapsed on a large rock, as far as possible from the others. His legs were cramping from the exertion, but he didn't have the strength to rub them. He was completely drained and too exhausted even to cry, let alone scream in anguish like the woman nearby who had just lost her son. She was walking in circles, carrying the burnt remains of the small body in her own scorched hands. Rodrigo could imagine how she must have plunged those hands into the boiling lava to rescue the boy. The odor of burnt flesh spiraled around her as she paced before the entrance to the cave. Outside, in the unbearable heat, everything was tinged with glowing lava.

Rodrigo closed his eyes at the sight, regretting his own escape. What was the point of fighting to survive in this place where he did not belong? Although he no longer remembered who he was or where he came from, he had a profound sense that he had once lived in a privileged moment. And now—bereft, racked with sorrow—he existed in an endless void. It seemed as though half his body had been ripped away. He didn't know what to do: there was no means of escape, and besides, where could he go? He had no family, no one even to weep for him. How long could he survive on this planet? On his own, not even a day, yet even as a member of this tribe he had scarcely any hope. He was constantly aware of the suspicious glances the savages directed at him. He could not blame them. He was male, but hairless and unaggressive; he lacked their brute strength; he possessed no scars; and furthermore, he had all his teeth—something unknown to an adult male on Korma. Instead of defecating in the cave, he would go outside and hide behind a tree; instead of attacking dinosaurs, he would use the tip of a spear to clean the dirt from his fingernails; instead of eating his nasal mucus, he would blow his nose with his fingers, covering his face with his other hand so that no one would see; and to top it off, he had never fornicated with any of the women of the tribe. All these things made him highly suspect and universally scorned.

Only one woman was attracted to him, and no one knew why. The fact was, she had been the only Kormian to witness the landing of the spacecraft that had brought Rodrigo to Korma. She had watched it descend from the heavens amid fire and thunder, and she had later seen Rodrigo, naked and confused, emerge from the strange device as from a floating womb. Thus for her, Rodrigo was some strange god born of the stars. More than once she had saved his life, defending him like a tigress against the other males of the clan, but she could not find a way to show him her feelings. Sometimes she would lie down before him and spread her hairy legs, in a clear invitation for him to mount her as other primitives did at the least provocation, but Rodrigo would pretend not to see her, and things would progress no further.

Still, this primitive woman had not lost faith and felt that, now that her god was wounded, she had her chance. Crouching at his feet, she tenderly began licking the wounds he had sustained escaping the flood of lava. He opened his eyes at her touch and attempted to draw back his feet, but his muscles would not obey. After a few seconds, he realized how soothing it was to feel her moist tongue stroking the burned soles of his feet. He felt so comforted that he set aside his resistance, closed his eyes, and allowed himself to enjoy it. The licking intensified as it proceeded upward. Occasionally the woman would pause to remove a thorn stuck in Rodrigo's leg, then she continued upward, past his knees, lingering over his thighs—where clearly there was no wound—until she finally arrived at her main objective: his groin. Lecherously, she licked her lips before continuing her labors. Rodrigo grew apprehensive. He knew very well what she wanted, this repulsive, hairy-chested woman who stank like a beast, had pestilent breath, and was lasciviously wiggling her ass. What she wanted was precisely what he had been avoiding from the start.

Fortunately, one of the primitive males had not missed a single bit of what was going on between them. Not for a second had he taken his eyes off the female's raised hindquarters: that she was on all fours made her even more desirable. Without a thought he grabbed her by the hips, and began fornicating with her. She grunted in protest and received in return a thump on the head that subdued her. Rodrigo, while grateful that the male had taken over, was disturbed by his methods. Since the woman had saved his life on several occasions, he felt obliged to return her favor. Not knowing from where, he found the strength to get to his feet and pull the male off her. The latter, enraged, lashed out with a wallop that left Rodrigo feeling as though he had been mauled by a dinosaur. Rodrigo could not take any more and burst into tears of impotence. What had he ever done to deserve such punishment? What crime was he paying for?

Everyone stared at him in amazement. His tears disillusioned even the female who had so greatly admired him. And from that moment on, he was unanimously shunned for being queer.

4

Dr. Díez's aerophone did not admit Azucena, an indication that he was occupied with a patient and had put a block on it. So Azucena had no choice but to go to her own office next door and from there make an appointment with her colleague, as she should have done in the first place. Azucena realized she had been wrong in keying in the doctor's aerophone number without calling first, but she had been so desperate that she had ignored the basic rules of courtesy. And what was technology for, if not to prevent people from forgetting their manners? So Azucena was forced to behave in a civilized fashion. As she waited for her office door to open, she realized she hadn't been there in a week and would be sure to have countless messages from all the patients she had abandoned.

The first thing Azucena heard as she entered her office was a collective "It's about time!" She was stunned, but then felt a pang of guilt. Her plants had just spent seven days without water, and so had every right to greet her this way. She always left them connected to the Plantspeaker, a device that translated their electrical emissions into words, because she liked hearing them welcome her each day when she arrived at work.

Ordinarily Azucena's plants were well behaved and extremely affectionate. They had never before spoken a harsh word to her. But Azucena could not bring herself to scold them, since she herself knew what it felt like to be left stranded. So before she did anything else, she watered them, pleading with them to forgive her, singing songs to them, caressing them as though she were the one being consoled. The plants soon calmed down and began purring with pleasure.

Azucena then played back her aerophone messages. The most pressing one came from a young man who was the reincarnation of a famous twentieth-century soccer player named Hugo Sánchez. Since 2200 the youth, once an athlete, had played for the Earth All-Stars, and with the Interplanetary Soccer Championship coming up soon, everyone was hoping he would be in top form. The problem was that his experiences as Hugo Sánchez had traumatized him; his teammates had been so jealous of him that they had made his life hell. As much as Azucena had worked with him during several astroanalytical sessions, she still could not completely erase the bitter experience of having been barred from playing in the 1994 World Cup.

The next message came from his wife, who in a previous life had been Dr. Mejía Barón, the trainer who had not permitted Hugo to play that year. The two had been brought together once again so that they could learn how to love, but Hugo still could not forgive her and would give her a thrashing at every opportunity. The woman couldn't take any more and begged Azucena to help her; if not, she was determined to kill herself.

There were also several calls from the youth's current trainer. He wanted his star player spiritually aligned in time for the Earth–Venus match, which was just around the corner. Azucena thought it best to give the trainer the name of one of her other patients, who was the reincarnation of Pelé, since at present she was in no condition to treat anyone. She was terribly sorry, but what could she do? That's how it was. In order to function as an astroanalyst, you had to be cleansed of all negative emotions, and Azucena clearly was not.

Before she could listen to the rest of her messages, she was interrupted by her plants, which were shrieking hysterically. Through the thin office wall, they had been listening to an argument coming from Dr. Díez's office, and they were jarred by its harsh vibrations. Azucena immediately went into the hall and knocked on Dr. Díez's door. The doctor was the most peaceful person she knew, so something awful must have been going on for him to explode like this.

Her knocking silenced the quarrel. No one came to the door, however, and she was about to knock again when suddenly the door flew open and a burly man shoved Azucena back against her own door, shattering the glass reading *Azucena Martínez, Astroanalyst*. After that man came a second, even more enraged, and after him Dr. Díez. At the sight of Azucena lying on the floor, he stopped in his tracks and rushed over to help her.

"Azucena! So it was you! Are you hurt?"

"I don't think so."

The doctor helped Azucena to her feet and quickly checked her over.

"You seem all right."

"But what about you? Did they hurt you?"

"No, we were just having a discussion. But it was lucky you came."

"Who were those men?"

"No one, no one important. But God, what's happened to you?"

"It's nothing, they just knocked me against the door."

"I don't mean that. What's the matter with *you?* Are you sick? You look awful."

Azucena could no longer hold back the tears. The doctor gave her a paternal hug, and Azucena, her voice choked with sobs, unburdened herself, telling him how she had found her twin soul, and how briefly that joy had lasted. How in one day she had gone from the tender bliss of her lover's embrace to a desolate, tormenting void. She told him how she had already searched everywhere, but still could find no trace of Rodrigo. Her only remaining hope was to locate him by means of Dr. Díez's new invention. As soon as Azucena mentioned the word "invention," the doctor became anxious, looking around him to be sure no one was listening. Then he took Azucena by the arm and led her into his office.

"Come along with me. We can talk better in here."

Azucena took one of the comfortable leather chairs facing the doctor's desk. Dr. Díez spoke in a low voice, as if someone might be listening.

"Look, Azucena, you're a good friend and I'd love to help you, but I can't."

Disappointment made Azucena mute. Her eyes misted with sadness.

"I put together only two machines. The police have one, and they would never lend it to me, because they're using it around the clock to find Mr. Bush's assassin. As for the second one, I can't let you have it either. I don't even have authorization to enter the Center for the Oversight of Previous Existences, where it is, although . . . Let me think. You know, there *is* an opening at COPE. Maybe if you got the job, you could use the machine on site."

"Are you kidding? They don't accept anybody but born and bred bureaucrats. There's no way they'd hire me."

"What if I have a way to help you become a bureaucrat?"

"You do? How?"

The doctor removed a tiny instrument from his desk drawer and showed it to Azucena.

"With this."

The female bureaucrat quickly put her tasty tamale back in the drawer and carefully wiped her fingers on her skirt before addressing Azucena Martínez, the final candidate she had to interview for the position of Official Investigator.

"Please have a seat."

"Thank you."

"I see you're an astroanalyst."

"Yes, I am."

"That's such a high-paying job . . . Why would you want to apply for a clerical position like this?"

Azucena felt extremely nervous. She knew a photomental camera was recording her every thought and she only hoped that the microcomputer Dr. Díez had installed in her brain was sending out thoughts of love and peace. If not, she was lost, for what she was really thinking right then was that interviews like this were a joke and that government offices were mired in crap.

"Well, you see, I'm emotionally exhausted, so my doctor recommended taking a break. My aura has been charged with negative energy and needs to recuperate. You know how it is . . . I work really long hours listening to all kinds of problems."

"Yes, I understand. Just as I'm sure you'll appreciate how important it is for us to have knowledge about a person's prior lives in order to know how they will conduct themselves in their work here."

"Of course."

"So I assume you'll have no objection to our directly examining your subconscious; this will enable us to reach our final conclusion as to whether or not you are suitably qualified to fill the position of Official Investigator."

Azucena felt cold sweat trickling down her back. She was frightened to the core, for now the test of fire awaited her. Although no one could delve into another person's subconscious without prior authorization, she would have to allow them to do so if she really wanted a job at COPE. Of course, she would never allow them access to her true subconscious, since the information the analysts were looking for concerned her moral and social integrity. They wanted to learn whether in any of her lives she had tortured or murdered someone, how honest she was at present, what kind of tolerance she had for frustration, or if she was likely to involve herself in some revolutionary movement. Azucena was very honest, and had already spent several lifetimes improving her karma, paying for sins she had committed in previous lives. However, her tolerance level for frustration was close to zero. She was a born agitator and rebel—all the more reason to hope that Dr. Díez's apparatus continued to work properly. If not, she would not only find herself without a job as Official Investigator, but would be dealt a more fatal blow: they would erase all trace of past lives from her memory, and that would really mean Good-bye, Rodrigo!

"What is your password?"

"Buried Potatoes."

The bureaucrat typed the words into the computer and handed Azucena a helmet containing a photomental camera that would record her subconscious thoughts, translating them into images of virtual reality. These in turn would be transmitted to the Data

Control Office, where they would be minutely analyzed by a team of scientists as well as a computer.

Azucena put on the helmet and closed her eyes; in a moment she was listening to some very pleasing music.

In the adjoining office, the Mexico City of 1985 was being reproduced in virtual reality. The scientific bureaucrats were thus able to walk along Avenida Samuel Ruiz just as it had been two hundred and fifteen years earlier, when it had been known as Eje Lázaro Cárdenas. They reached the Metropolitan Cathedral, which looked just as it had before it was damaged, and continued along Eje Central, arriving at Plaza de Garibaldi, where they stopped beside a group of mariachis playing for some passing tourists.

A heated discussion ensued among the scientists over the clarity of the images they were viewing. Ordinarily, the mind recalls events in a confused and disorganized way. Azucena was the first person they had seen who recalled every detail of her past with such precision. The images she projected followed a perfect sequence. They were not at all fragmented, which suggested that either this girl was a genius, or she had illegally slipped in a micro-computer. One scientist suggested notifying the police. Several others favored an internal investigation. The remaining ones, however, moved by the sound of the mariachi trumpets, were reduced to tears.

Fortunately in these cases, there is only one whose opinion holds any weight, only one who can render the final verdict: the computer. And the computer accepted without hesitation the information provided by Azucena. The opinion of the scientists was taken into account only when the computer failed to function, and this had happened only once in the past hundred and fifty years, during the time of the Great Earthquake, when the Earth gave birth to the New Moon. And at that time no one was interested in scientific opinion because all that mattered was saving one's skin.

Azucena meanwhile, completely isolated from everyone, was listening to the music coming from the audiophones in her helmet. She felt as though she were literally floating in time as the melody gently transported her to one of her past lives. Her true subconscious had begun to work spontaneously, bringing forth an image she had seen once during an astroanalysis session. She had never been able to get beyond it, because something was blocking that past life from her; but evidently the melody she now heard had the power to break through that barrier.

CD
Track 1

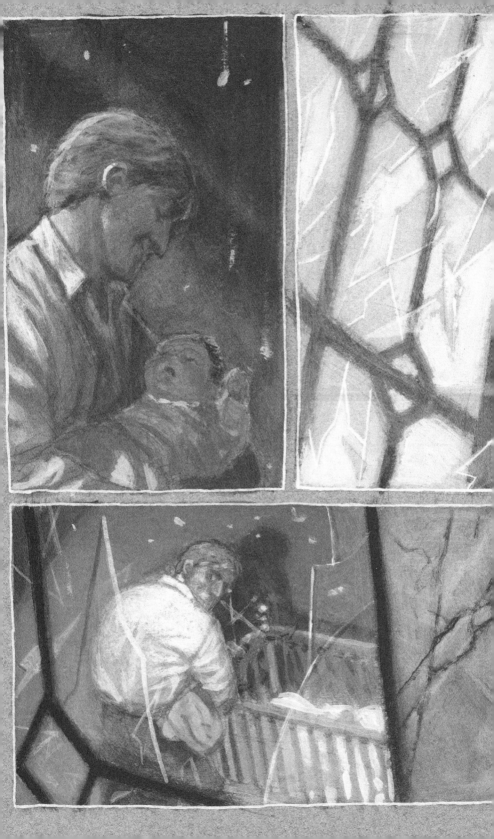

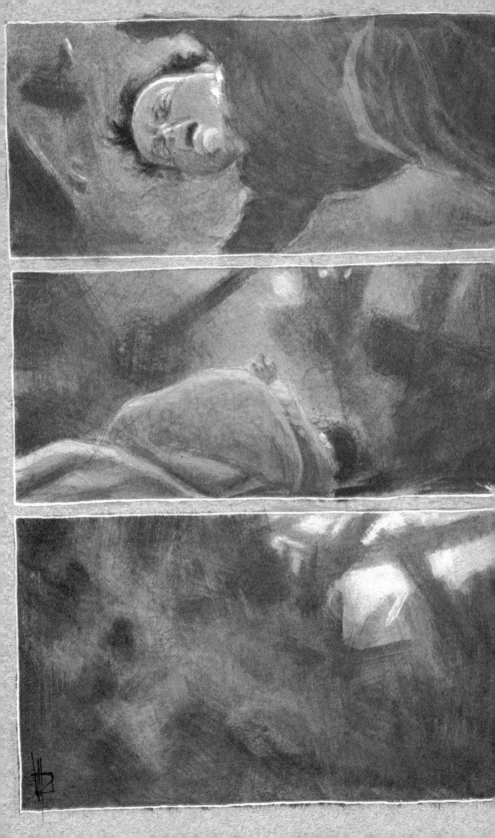

Suddenly the music stopped, leaving Azucena's mind blank. Her helmet had been disconnected. How could the bureaucrat be waking her just when she saw Rodrigo? Azucena was absolutely certain Rodrigo was that man who had scooped her into his arms from the cradle and saved her life. She recognized his face as one of the fourteen thousand from his previous lives, which she had seen on the day they met. She hadn't the slightest doubt. It was Rodrigo! She must know what that music was that had led her to him.

"That will be all, thank you. Now we'll have to wait for the final decision."

"That music I was listening to, what was it?"

"Classical music."

"Yes, I know, but who wrote it?"

"I don't know, seems to me it's from an opera, but I'm not sure."

"Do you think you could find out?"

"Why are you so interested in it?"

"Oh, it's not that I'm interested personally. But in my work as an astroanalyst it's very useful to be familiar with music that can induce altered states of consciousness."

"I can imagine. But since you won't be working as an astroanalyst for some time, it hardly matters."

Through a slit in the desk, the computer spit out a sheet of paper. The bureaucrat read it and then handed it to Azucena.

"Hmmm. Congratulations, you passed the exam. Just take this paper to the second floor. They'll take an aurograph there for your ID. As soon as you have it, you can report for work."

Azucena was beside herself with joy. She couldn't believe how lucky she had been. Although she tried to hide her emotions, she could not suppress a smile of triumph. Everything was working out perfectly. She'd show that Anacreonte how to solve problems!

On the second floor, there were about five hundred people waiting to have their aurographs taken. This was nothing compared to the endless lines Azucena had stood in before, so she took her place at the end of this one with the usual resignation. Meanwhile a photomental camera was constantly scanning all of them as a final test, registering the frustration tolerance of these future bureaucrats. It turned out that her fellow applicants in line had what it takes to be bureaucrats and easily withstood the test. Azucena did not. Each passing minute sapped her patience. The nervous tapping of her heel on the floor was the first thing to raise the eyebrows of the qualifying judges. It completely contradicted the thoughts she was emitting. The photomental camera focused on her face, capturing her impatient frown. The total disparity between Azucena's thoughts and her appearance was highly suspicious. This may have been why the moment she reached the window to be helped, the "Closed" sign went up. Azucena's blood was boiling. This couldn't be! She *couldn't* have such bad luck. She had to bite her lip so she wouldn't scream obscenities; shut her eyes so they wouldn't release the daggers she wanted to bury in the woman's throat; clamp her feet together so she wouldn't kick the window to smithereens; knot her fingers to keep them from shredding to bits all these papers they were handing her as they told her to return next Monday.

Monday! And it was only Thursday morning now. She couldn't just sit around waiting for Monday to come. But what *could* she do? She would have loved to continue that regression to the past life where she had seen Rodrigo, but she didn't know the name of the opera they had been playing and, even if she did, it wouldn't be easy to obtain. The latest discoveries in music therapy had complicated the sale and purchase of CDs. It had been known for some time that musical sounds have a powerful influence on the human organism and can alter psychological states, inducing at times neurotic, schizophrenic, psychopathic, and—in extreme cases—even murderous behavior.

Recently, however, it had been discovered that a single melody had the power to activate our memory of past lives. Music was currently being used in the area of astroanalysis to induce regressions to former incarnations. As might be expected, it was not appropriate that just anyone use music for these purposes, since not everyone had achieved the same stage of evolution. Sometimes it was thought best not to lift the lid on the past, for if an awareness was blocked, it was usually because the person in question was not ready to deal with it. There had been too many times when, for example, a former king had sought to recover jewels from a crown belonging to him in a past incarnation—things of that sort. So the government had decreed that all records, stereos, cassettes, CDs, and other audio equipment should fall under the jurisdiction of the Director of Public Health. If you wanted to buy a CD, you had to demonstrate your moral integrity and your level of spiritual development by presenting a certified letter from an astroanalyst stating that the holder would not be running any risk by listening to the music in question.

As an astroanalyst, Azucena could cut through that red tape without difficulty, but it would take nearly a month to do so. And that would be an eternity! She had to think of another way, because if she went back to her apartment without making some progress in locating Rodrigo, she would go mad. She wanted to see him face to face, and as soon as possible, to find out why he had abandoned her. Had she done something wrong? Wasn't she attractive enough? Or did he have another lover whom he could not abandon? Azucena was prepared to accept any explanation, but she wanted to hear it coming from his lips.

What she couldn't bear was all this uncertainty. It reawakened in her all the insecurities she had worked so hard to overcome through astroanalysis. Her lack of self-confidence had prevented her from forming a stable relationship in the past. Whenever she had found someone worthwhile who treated her well, she had invariably ended up breaking it off. Deep down, she had always felt she didn't deserve happiness; yet she still had had a profound need to feel loved. It was in an effort to resolve these problems that she had decided to find her twin soul, thinking that with him she couldn't go wrong. It had taken so long to find him! And then to have lost him so soon! It was the greatest injustice she had suffered in all her fourteen thousand lives.

Azucena knew she had better do something fast to assuage all this anguish and considered that her best bet would be to go stand in line at the Consumer Protection Agency. There at least she could pick a fight with somebody, or simply complain, scream, demand her rights. The bureaucrats on duty in such places were among the most forbearing of government employees, having been assigned there expressly so that people could take out their frustrations on them. Yes, that was what she would do.

The Consumer Protection Agency looked like the anteroom to Hell. Complaints, laments, and tears filled the stifling room, where thousands of people stood crammed together. By the time Azucena made her way to the line for Twin Souls, she was drenched in sweat. So was Cuquita, who was standing a few feet away. Cuquita! There was the super from Azucena's building, in the Astral Ascension line right next to her. They both pretended they had not seen each other, for the last thing they wanted was to have to speak. But fate seemed determined to bring them together, because the moment Cuquita reached the window,

Azucena moved up in line and found herself nearly elbow to elbow with her.

From where she stood she could not avoid hearing all of Cuquita's conversation with the bureaucrat. Communication between the two was complicated by Cuquita's repeated efforts to impress the woman by using language she considered elegant and cultivated. However, since she didn't know what half the terms meant, she only ended up annoying the clerk.

"Listen, Señorita. You have any idea how meretricious I've been?"

"I beg your pardon?"

"I've levitated my soul high enough to merit scatological treatment."

"I'm sure you have, Señora, but the problem is you have to pay for everything in life, either in installments or cash on the barrel-head—but you still have to pay."

"I know, but look, I've paid off my karmic dues, verbatim. And now I want my divorce."

"I'm very sorry, Señora, but our records indicate that you still owe outstanding debts to your husband from prior lives."

"What debts?"

"Do I need to remind you of your life as a film critic?"

"Well, okay, I admit I was pretty nasty, but not enough to deserve this! I've spent enough time paying off karmas from posterior lives not to be stuck with a man guilty of default and battery. Just look at this eye! If you don't grant me a divorce soon, I swear I'll kill him."

"Do what you like, but you'll still have to pay. Next, please."

"Look, isn't there some way we can work this out between us, so that I can meet my twin soul?"

"No, Señora, it won't work. Let me tell you, lots of people are in the same boat. They all want beauty, money, health, or fame—

without ever doing anything to deserve them. But still, if you really want to go ahead and meet your twin soul without earning the privilege, we can always work out a credit. That is, assuming you're willing to pay interest."

"How much interest are we talking about?"

"If you sign this form, we can put you in touch with your twin soul in less than a month, but you'll have to commit to spending ten more lives with your current husband, taking beatings, humiliation, whatever he chooses to dish out. If you agree to this, we can arrange it immediately."

"No way!"

"Well, here we go again . . . People are willing to ask for anything, but they're never interested in paying up. I suggest you think about what you really want to do."

Azucena was embarrassed to have overheard Cuquita's complaints. Although she didn't like Cuquita, still she didn't enjoy seeing her suffer, and the worst of it was that Azucena knew poor Cuquita didn't stand a chance of meeting her twin soul at present. Who could tell how many more lives she would have to wait? By this time Azucena had come to believe that love and waiting were one and the same. Love always meant waiting, yet love, paradoxically, spurred her to action because waiting kept her going. Azucena's love for Rodrigo had caused her to stand in countless lines, to lose weight, to purify her body and soul. But his disappearance had prevented her from thinking about anything that wasn't connected with learning his whereabouts. She had let herself go. She didn't care whether her hair was combed or her teeth brushed. She didn't even care whether or not her aura was luminous. Nothing that happened was of any importance unless it could be related to Rodrigo.

All this while, the person behind her in the line had been telling her about his past lives, but Azucena had not really heard a word of it, although it had nearly put her to sleep. The man hadn't noticed, because Azucena's face kept the same neutral expression throughout his monologue, and to look at her, you could never tell she was about to drift off to sleep. This man was the perfect cure for the galloping insomnia that had plagued her ever since Rodrigo disappeared. She had tried everything, from linden-flower tea to warm milk and honey, to her foolproof method of remembering all the lines she had stood on in her lifetime. The trick was to count backward, one by one, every person who had been at a window before her. This method had never failed until she lost Rodrigo. Now each time she thought of a line, she would remember how hopeful she had been as she stood there, dreaming about being kissed and caressed . . . and then sleep was frightened away once and for all. But now—maybe it was the combination of the heat and her companion's chatter, for this man could numb an entire battalion—the truth was, she was about to fall asleep on her feet.

"And did I tell you about my life as a ballerina?"

"No, I don't think so."

"Well, in that life . . . It's funny how things turn out. I didn't want to be a ballerina, I wanted to be a musician, but since I'd been a rock star in a previous life and had made quite a few people deaf with my racket, they wouldn't hear of giving me a good ear again, so I had no choice but to be a ballerina. But I don't regret it—it turned out to be great! That is, except for the bunions I got from those toe shoes. But all in all, I still loved dancing on pointe. It felt like floating, like floating on air . . . like . . . like— Oh, I don't know how to explain it. But the worst thing was, they killed me off when I was only twenty years old. Can you believe it? Oh, it was awful! I was just leaving the theater one night when some men tried to rape me; I fought back, and one of them killed me."

Azucena softened a little at the sight of this big ugly man crying like a little kid. She gave him her handkerchief to dry his tears, and tried to imagine him dancing on pointe, but failed.

"It was really unfair, because I was pregnant . . . and I never got to see my baby. . . ."

He had pronounced the crucial phrase to capture Azucena's attention: "I never got to see my baby." If there was one thing Azucena knew, it was the pain of losing someone. She immediately identified with the sorrow of this poor man, who never got to see the little creature he had so loved and waited for. She could find no way of consoling him; she could only gaze at him with sympathetic eyes.

"That's why I came here, to file a complaint. I was due a woman's body in this life to finish my apprenticeship in the other life, but by mistake I was born in this nightmare of a body. Pretty ugly, isn't it?"

Azucena wanted to cheer him up, but she couldn't think of a single pleasantry. This man's ugliness seemed like a slap in the face to God.

"Oh, you don't know what I'd give to look like you. I hate having a man's body. And since I don't really like women, I have to have homosexual relationships. But most men are brutes! They don't know how to be tender with me, and that's what I crave. Oh, if I were only slender and delicate, then they'd treat me gently."

"Haven't you ever asked for a soul transplant?"

"Are you kidding! I've been standing in lines like this for ten years, but each time there's a body available, they give it to somebody else, never me. I'm desperate."

"Well, I hope they give you one soon."

"So do I."

The man returned the handkerchief Azucena had lent him. She took it gingerly by one corner, because he had liberally blown his nose in it, but then decided to give it back to him rather than put it in her purse. He thanked her warmly and then hurriedly said good-bye, because it was almost Azucena's turn at the window.

"You're next, so thanks, and good luck!"

"You, too."

"Next?"

Azucena approached the window.

"Uh, look, Señorita . . . You see, they processed my documents in Astral Ascension a long time ago."

"All Ascension affairs are in that line over there. Next."

"Listen, let me finish. They told me there that I was ready to meet my twin soul; they put me in touch with him, and we actually met."

"If you've already met him, what are you doing here? Your problem's been solved. Next . . ."

"No, wait! I'm not through! The problem is that he just disappeared, overnight, and I can't find him. Can you provide me with his address?"

"What? You met him, but you don't know his address?"

"No, because all they gave me was his aerophone number. I already left a message for him, and he came to my house."

"Well, call him again. Next . . ."

"Come on, you must think I'm some kind of idiot, right? I've called him day and night, but no answer. And I can't go to his house because I'm not registered in his aerophone. Will you please give me his address—or would you rather have me create a scene? Because, believe me, I'm not leaving here without that address! You tell me whether it's going to be the easy way or the hard way."

Azucena's shouting was accompanied by a threatening glare that succeeded in terrorizing the bureaucrat. With great meekness, she took the paper Azucena handed her, read Rodrigo's particulars, and diligently searched for information on him in the computer.

"No such person exists."

"What do you mean, he doesn't exist?"

"I mean he doesn't exist. I've searched all the files under Embodied and Disembodied, and he doesn't show up on any list."

"That's not possible, he *has* to be there."

"I tell you, *he doesn't exist.*"

"Look, Señorita, please don't give me that crap! I'm living proof he exists, because I'm his twin soul. Rodrigo Sánchez exists because I exist. Period!"

Not a single person in the entire Consumer Protection Agency was spared from Azucena's shrieking, but no one was more shocked by it than her companion in the line. Even after Azucena in her fury had swept up her papers from the counter and turned to leave, he still stood there, not knowing whether to step up to the window for his turn, or to follow Azucena out the door.

As she left the building, Azucena felt a tap on her shoulder that made her jump. She turned to see a shady-looking character whispering something to her.

"Need a body?"

"A what?"

"A body—I can get you one in excellent condition and at a good price."

This was just what she needed to top off her memorable morning in the realm of bureaucracy. She had made the mistake of answering this *coyote*, and that was enough to make him stick to her like a leech for several blocks at least. These kinds of characters were always seen hanging around outside government office buildings. You had to ignore them completely if you wanted to walk down the street in peace, because as soon as they noticed you observing them, even for a second out of the corner of your eye, they insisted on pushing their services on you.

"No thank you."

"Come on, you won't get a better price anywhere."

"I said no! I don't need a body."

"Well, I don't want to say so, but yours looks a little beat up."

"What's that to you!"

"Okay, I'll shut up, but . . . Come on, we just got some new ones in, really beautiful—blue eyes and all. . . ."

"I don't want any!"

"What can you lose, just taking a look?"

"I said no! Do you understand?"

"If you're worried about the cops, let me tell you, we only deal in bodies with no registered auras."

"I'm not worried about the police, I'm going to *call* them, if you don't stop being such a damn pest!"

"Oooh, what a temper!"

It hadn't gone too badly; it had only taken a block and a half at top speed to shake him off. At the corner, Azucena looked back to be sure he still wasn't following her, and spotted him bearing down on the "ballerina" instead. She hoped that in his desperation to have a woman's body he wouldn't fall into the clutches of the *coyote*. But for the time being, she had too many problems of her own to worry about. From now on, the world could fall apart before her eyes and she wouldn't care. She walked along, so involved in her thoughts that she did not even notice the spacecraft circling the city to announce the nomination of a new candidate for Planetary President: Isabel González.

INTERMISSION FOR DANCING

CD
Track 2

Bad because you don't love me
Bad because you never touch me
Bad because you have a mouth
Bad whenever you please

Bad as lies
Bad breath, constipation
Bad as censorship
As a bald rat in garbage
Bad as poverty
As a driver's license photo
Bad as a rubber check
As smacking your granny

Bad as trichinosis
Bad as a hit man
Bad as spiders
Bad and full of cunning

Bad as order, decency, or a good conscience
Bad wherever you look
Bad as a throbbing root canal
Bad as a rusty nail
Bad as a Czech film
Bad as cold soup
Bad as the end of the century

Bad by nature
Bad from head to foot
Bad, bad, bad
Bad, but so damn beautiful

LILIANA FELIPE

5

Being a Demon is an enormous responsibility, but being Mammon, Isabel's Demon, is truly a blessing; for Isabel González is the best student I've had in millions of years.

She is the most beautiful flower of meekness ever to blossom in the fields of power and ambition. Her soul has yielded to my counsel with profound innocence, and without any doubts: she takes my suggestions as orders, and carries them out instantly. No one—nothing—stands in her way. She eliminates whatever must be eliminated without a trace of remorse. So persistent is she in attaining her goals that she will soon be made part of our collegiate league, and on that day I shall be the proudest devil in all Hell.

I consider myself fortunate to have been chosen as her teacher. After all, they could have selected any one of the other fallen angels that inhabit these shadowy domains, many of whom have better teaching credentials than I have. But, thank God, I was the lucky one. And thanks to Isabel's diligence, I'm going to earn the promotion I've been waiting for all these centuries. Finally I shall be given the recognition I deserve, because up until now I've received nothing but ingratitude. All that hard work for such little pay! The ones who have always carried off all the applause, all the medals and glory, are the Guardian Angels. I ask myself, where would they be without us Demons?

An evolving spirit must pass through every imaginable horror before reaching enlightenment, for there is no way of arriving at light except through darkness. A soul is tempered only by suffering and pain. There is no way for human beings to avoid this predicament, nor is it useful to give them lessons in advance. The human soul is basically very stupid and cannot comprehend an experience until it lives it out in the flesh. Likewise, no knowledge ever reaches the brain without first passing through the organs of the senses.

Before realizing it was wrong to eat the forbidden fruit, man first had to experience its enticing scent; to anticipate the delight of biting into its flesh, of hearing its skin give way, of savoring each morsel, sensing its contours, its succulence, its gentle caresses as it makes its way through the esophagus, the stomach, the intestines. Not until Adam ate the apple did his mind open to new knowledge. Only when his intestines digested it, did his brain comprehend that he was walking around naked in Paradise. Not until he suffered the consequences of partaking in the wisdom of the God who created him did he realize his transgression. Simply telling him not to eat of the Tree of Good and Evil would never have been enough. There is no way for human beings to accept a priori a line of reasoning; they have to live it out in all its fullness.

And who is it who provides these opportunities? The Guardian Angels? Hell, no! It is we, the Demons, who do it. Thanks to our labors, man suffers. Thanks to all the trials we subject him to, he is able to evolve. And what do we get in return? Rejection, ingratitude, bad press. What else is new? Our role in life has always been to play the part of the bad guys. After all, someone has to do it. Someone has to be the teacher, the discipliner, man's guide through the murky darkness. And I can tell you, it is not easy. To educate is to fight a constant battle, administering pain, suffering, punishment, without relief. It is sheer torment to watch man continually suffer—all because of us.

And it doesn't help knowing it's for their own good, because that knowledge does not alleviate their agony. How I would love to be one of those who give relief, who console, who dry the tears, who offer the protective embrace. But then, who would push man to evolve? Someone has to wield the whip. What would become of a piano if nobody ever struck its keys? We would never hear the unique tones it is capable of sounding.

Sometimes you have to do violence to matter in order to reveal its beauty. The blows of a chisel convert a block of marble into a masterpiece. We must know how to strike without pity, without remorse, without fear of discarding the bits of stone that stand in the way of its splendor. To know how to produce a work of art is to know how to discard the extraneous. All creation follows the same process. In the maternal womb, the cells themselves know what to discard; some sacrifice themselves so that others may exist. In order for the upper lip to separate from the lower, thousands of cells that once joined them must die. Were that not so, how could man speak, sing, eat, kiss, or sigh with love?

The soul, unfortunately, is not as wise as those cells. It is merely a diamond in the rough, which must abide the blows inflicted by suffering in order to shine in all its brilliance. You would think it might learn to stop resisting punishment. But it will not consent to be the cell that commits suicide so the mouth can open and speak for us all; human beings never want to be the piece that is chiseled away to reveal the work of art. So, there is no recourse but to slough some of them off for the benefit of all humanity.

The ones chosen to perform these necessary acts are those who inflict violence: those who respect neither the place nor the order of things. Those who have no awe of life, who never stop to marvel at the beauty of the evening sky; those who know that the world can always be changed to their advantage; that there are no boundaries that cannot be encroached upon, no order that cannot be undone, no law that cannot be rewritten, no virtue that cannot be bought, no body that cannot be possessed, no sacred text that cannot be burned, no pyramid that cannot be destroyed, no opponent that cannot be assassinated.

Such persons are our strongest allies, and, among them all, Isabel reigns queen: the most merciless, ambitious, cruel, and sublimely obedient of all the violators. Her brutal blows, struck with such virtuosity, have produced the most extraordinary music. Thanks to the tortures she inflicted, there were many who received Lucifer's benedictions; thanks to the wars she provoked, great advances were made in science and technology. Because she practiced corruption, men found themselves able to exercise generosity; due to her abuses of the privileges of power, her lack of respect, her obstinacy, her need to control every act of her subordinates, many were finally able to achieve enlightenment and knowledge.

A person can learn the value of his legs only when they've been cut off. To appreciate solidarity, one must first be an outcast. To learn to value order, one must first feel the effects of chaos. Thus if a man is to value life in the universe, he must first learn to destroy it: to regain Paradise, he must first regain Hell, *and above all, he must love it.* For it is only by loving what we despise that we evolve. The only way to arrive at God is by means of the Devil. So Azucena should be very grateful to be included in the destiny of my precious Isabel, for soon, very soon, it will bring her into contact with God.

6

Let us rejoice, Oh friends,
And embrace each other here.
Now we walk on the flowering earth.
No one here need put an end
To flowers or songs.
They will live on in the house of the
    Giver of Life.

This earth is the realm of the fleeting
    moment.
Is it the same, as well, in that region
Where somehow one still exists?
Is one happy there?
Is there friendship there?
Or is it only here on earth
That we come to know our faces?

AYOCUAN CUETZPALTZIN
Trece Poetas del Mundo Azteca
MIGUEL LEÓN-PORTILLA

As Isabel's house filled up with flowers and congratulatory faxes, her heart was seized with fear. Life could not have granted her a greater prize than being chosen as the Americas' candidate for Planetary President. She had finally attained her dream of reaching the heights of power and gaining the respect and admiration of all. But now she was terrified. A mounting fear prevented her from enjoying her triumph. The more that people showed their support, the more threatened she felt, for she knew that any number of them would love to be in her shoes. Realizing how she was envied and closely watched only made her feel more vulnerable. She considered everyone around her a potential enemy and began taking extreme precautions. Knowing that human beings are by nature corruptible, she trusted no one. Anybody might betray her. She slept with her door locked, was constantly detecting strange odors that only she seemed to notice, and had become hypersensitive to tastes as well. In short, she sensed an imminent physical danger and was convinced the entire world was plotting against her.

As long as she had had nothing to lose, she had lived a tranquil existence, but now that she was on the verge of having it all, she was shaky as a poppy in the wind. She felt the way she had as a child, when she refused to walk in the dark for fear that the bogeyman would jump out at her. She had the same sensation even when watching love scenes in movies, for she knew that they usually preceded disasters. So instead of enjoying the lovers' kisses, she was anxiously scanning the screen, anticipating the moment when the dagger would come into view and be thrust into the man's back. It was the same with film music: she knew frightening music always accompanied horror; so instead of enjoying the love theme she was always listening for the slightest variation in its melody, so she could shut her eyes and avoid the jolt to her soul.

Anyone knew that this kind of constant strain was bad for one's health. The Department of Public Health and Welfare had gone so far as to prohibit suspense music in films, which had been linked to liver damage in spectators. Isabel herself had enthusiastically endorsed the measure. Her only regret was that there wasn't a similar organization to regulate the intrusion of tragedies into everyday life, some means of preventing the fact that from one moment to the next you could pass from wedding bells to an ambulance's wail; some way of warning people when something terrible was approaching, so that she would be able to shut her eyes in time. The situation Isabel found herself in was stretching her nerves to the limit. Everyone wanted to see her, interview her, be close to her—close, that is, to power. She had to meet every situation head-on, with her eyes wide open, be extremely vigilant, trust no one, not leave the tiniest loose end dangling so that one of her enemies could use it to destroy her. She had to be on the alert and to steel her heart whenever necessary. Although she had no problem there: she had already shown herself capable of eliminating her own daughter, so she certainly could do the same to anybody else who got in her way.

That daughter had been born in Mexico City on January 12, 2180, at 21 hours, 20 minutes, under the sign of Capricorn, with Virgo in the ascendant. Her astrological chart indicated she would have many problems with authority due to the opposition of Saturn and Uranus, Saturn representing authority and Uranus, liberty and rebellion. In addition, the position of Uranus in the sign of Aries indicated extreme assertiveness, so that when this girl decided to be stubborn, she would be singleminded about it, if not impulsive and irresponsible. The position of Uranus in the eighth house suggested that she might become involved in shady dealings in her desire to challenge authority.

With all the subversive traits predicted by this chart, it was almost a given that the girl would grow up to be a perennial thorn in the side, especially for Isabel, who had always planned on becoming Planetary President. And this was not just some pipe dream of hers, for Isabel's astrological chart indicated it as well, predicting further that when this occurred, an era of peace would finally be established for all humanity. With this knowledge, Isabel did not want to have her own daughter impeding her. So before she could begin to feel any affection for the child, she ordered her to be disintegrated for one hundred years, so as not to thwart the destiny of the human race.

From time to time Isabel thought about that daughter. What would she have been like? Would she have been pretty? Would she have looked like her mother? Would she have been slender? Or fat like Carmela, her other daughter? Now that she thought of it, perhaps it would have been a good idea to have had Carmela disintegrated as well. All she ever did was embarrass Isabel. Just like this morning. The first thing Isabel had done upon awakening was to turn on the Televirtual for the broadcast of the interview she'd given following her nomination. She found it very pleasing to watch herself in virtual reality in her own bedroom. How thrilling to think that she had been in houses all over the world. She was told she had been seen by millions of viewers. The only problem was that Abel Zabludowsky had come up with the bright idea of interviewing Carmela. How embarrassing! Her pig of a daughter had also been in all those homes. She just hoped they had found some way of squeezing Carmela in without crowding her own image out. Talk about hogging the camera! She wondered what people thought of her. That she was a terrible mother not to put her daughter on a diet? What a nightmare! She didn't know what she should do about Carmela. And today Isabel was expecting crowds of people to stop by and fawn over her. Preparations were already under way for a press luncheon on the patio. She certainly didn't want her daughter to be anywhere in sight. But how could she hide her? Now that Carmela had been on the news, they'd all be asking about her. She had to come up with something. Her thoughts were interrupted by her daughter's voice.

"Mommy, may I come in?"

"Yes."

The door opened and there was Carmela, all dressed up for the luncheon. She had chosen a beautiful white lace dress because she wanted to look her best on such a special day for her mother.

"Get that dress off!"

"But . . . it's the nicest one I have."

"It's atrocious. You look like an overstuffed tamale. How in the world could you ever choose white, being as fat as you are?"

"But it's a luncheon, and you've always told me black is only for evening."

"You remember what I tell you well enough when it suits *you*, don't you? Try suiting *me* for a change. Get on another dress! And when you come back, show me the purse you'll be using, too, so I can see if it goes with your dress."

"I don't have a black bag."

"Then go find one somewhere! I don't want you coming down without a purse. Only whores parade around like that. Is that what you want, to look like a slut? Is that what you had in mind? To make a complete fool out of me?"

"No."

Carmela could not hold back her tears any longer. Extracting a tissue from her pocket, she dabbed at the stream running down her cheeks.

"What is *that?* Don't you have a handkerchief? How could you think of going anywhere without one? When have you ever seen a princess blowing her nose in a tissue? From now on, I want you to learn to behave appropriately for the daughter of someone in my position. Now get out of here, you make me furious!"

Carmela turned to leave, but before she reached the door, Isabel stopped her.

"And remember to keep out of range of the cameras."

Isabel was outraged. She was sick of dealing with young people. They always wanted to have their own way, disobey, impose their own wishes, challenge authority—that is, challenge *her*. She didn't understand why she always had the same effect on everyone. They couldn't see her as their superior without immediately wanting to rebel. Well, right now she needed to see if her employees had set up the patio exactly as she had told them.

The patio resembled a frenetic beehive, with countless workers scurrying all over the place under the direction of Agapito, Isabel's right-hand man. Agapito had had to work more frantically than ever to please his boss, because, considering the importance of the function, she'd given him almost no time to organize it. Isabel hadn't any reason for holding a press luncheon so soon. Her nomination had only been announced the day before, so nobody could have expected her to be prepared to have so many people; but she wanted to impress everyone with her organization. Agapito had taken charge with great efficiency, to assure that everything was perfect. The tables, tablecloths, floral arrangements, wines, food, service, invitations, press, music—all had been coordinated personally by him. No detail escaped him. He had at his fingertips the press clippings concerning the nomination, as well as a list of everyone who had called to congratulate Isabel. He knew only too well that the first thing she would want to know was who was on her side—and, by default, who was not, so that she could have them placed on her list of enemies.

As soon as he saw Isabel approach, Agapito felt a surge of apprehension. Having exerted himself to the fullest so that everything would be just right, he was in sore need of his boss's approval. Isabel glanced around the patio. Everything seemed to be in order, but then suddenly her eye was drawn to the center of the patio, where the remains of an ancient pyramid had poked up through the tiles. It was not the first time this problem had occurred. Now again Isabel had to remind them to cover it up, since it would not be at all convenient for the government to find out her house was sitting atop a pre-Hispanic pyramid. In such cases the State invariably ended up nationalizing the property. Then archeologists would arrive on the scene to begin their excavations, and, in the process, they would be likely to unearth a part of Isabel's past she preferred to keep buried deep beneath the earth.

"Agapito! Why haven't they covered the pyramid?"

"Well . . . we thought it'd be good for your image if people saw your concern for our pre-Hispanic past . . ."

"*We* thought? Who's 'we'?"

"Well, the boys and I . . ."

"The boys! The boys are idiots who can't think for themselves—they're supposed to follow *your* orders. If you can't control them, then what good are you? I'll just have to hire somebody who can make them obey."

"They obey me. It was my decision . . ."

"Then you're fired."

"But . . . why?"

"*Why?* Because I'm sick and tired of playing schoolteacher to a bunch of morons. I've told you a million times, anyone who doesn't do as I say can get the hell out!"

"But I did everything you told me to . . ."

"I never told you to leave that pyramid exposed."

"But you didn't say to cover it, either. It's not fair to fire me for one slipup. Everything else is perfect, you can see for yourself . . ."

"The only thing I see is that you're not a professional, so I want you out of here right now. Tell Rosalío to take over."

"Rosalío isn't here."

"Not here? Where did he go?"

"Downtown."

Isabel brightened at this news, and whispered to Agapito, "To get my chocolate?"

"No, you gave him permission to take his papers to the Consumer Protection Agency."

"Well, fire him, too. I'm fed up with both of you!"

Isabel cut short her screaming and put on her most charming smile the second she saw Abel Zabludowsky arriving with his cameras and crew. She was terrified. Had he heard her screaming? God, she hoped not. That would kill her image for sure. Just in case, she patted Agapito on the back to give the impression she'd been joking with him. Then her heart nearly froze as she saw Carmela steaming in, all six hundred sixty pounds of her. Isabel had to prevent Abel Zabludowsky from interviewing her again, let alone spotting the protruding pyramid.

Agapito was sharp enough to divine Isabel's thoughts, and came up with a brilliant solution that won him back his job and completely restored Isabel's former confidence in him.

"What if we sit Carmela right there on top of the pyramid, and tell her to stay put?"

And thus it was that the voluminous Carmela, black bag in hand, came to the rescue, preventing anyone from discovering that in the midst of her mother's patio a pyramid was about to be born.

7

Azucena walked home. Walking always restored her tranquillity. When she arrived at her corner, she saw Cuquita entering their building. Azucena was surprised to see her coming back so late, since she had left the Consumer Protection Agency long before Azucena. When she spotted the large bag Cuquita was carrying, Azucena realized that she must have gone shopping before returning home.

Cuquita, in turn, had caught sight of Azucena on the other side of the street, and seemed not at all pleased. She obviously wanted to get inside as quickly as possible to avoid meeting Azucena, but she found this difficult because her fat, drunken husband was sprawled across the doorway. Nothing unusual about that. Cuquita's husband was practically an architectural fixture in the neighborhood, and no one was surprised anymore when they saw him stretched out on the stairs, covered with vomit and flies. The neighbors had already filed a complaint with Health and Welfare, and Cuquita had been notified that she could not go on letting her spouse use the street as a bedroom.

Poor Cuquita! thought Azucena. No wonder she wanted to change husbands! On the other hand, she must have done something in her other lives to end up with karma like this. Azucena watched as Cuquita tried to drag her husband inside the building; he woke up, enraged, and began giving her an awful beating. This type of injustice always infuriated Azucena. It made her blood boil, and turned her into a force unleashed by nature. In an instant she was beside the mismatched pair. Grabbing Cuquita's husband by his hair, she slammed him against the wall and gave him a kick in the crotch. Then for good measure she added a right hook to the kidneys and, once he was on the ground, finished off with a flurry of kicks to vent all her remaining rage. Azucena ended up exhausting herself, but felt a great sense of relief.

Cuquita didn't know whether to kiss Azucena in gratitude or to gather up the contents of her shopping bag, which had spilled down the stairs. She decided to make her thanks brief and then rushed to collect the scattered articles before anyone noticed them. As Azucena leaned down to help, she was surprised to discover that the bag had been filled not with groceries but with an impressive assortment of Virtual Reality Books.

Some months before, Cuquita had asked Azucena for help in obtaining some of these VRBs for her blind grandmother, who was depressed about not being able to read or watch Televirtual. The VRB was a sensational device that had just come on the market. It consisted of a pair of spectacles that bypassed the eyes altogether, allowing the blind to "see" films in virtual reality with the same clarity as people who had vision. Cuquita's grandmother had been the first to put in a request for the apparatus, and the first to be rejected. She was not eligible for such indulgences because her blindness was karmic: as a former member of the Chilean military she had blinded several prisoners during torture.

Cuquita, however, seeing her grandmother weeping day and night, had worked up the nerve to ask Azucena for a letter of recommendation stating that she was the grandmother's astroanalyst, and could certify that the old woman had already paid off her bad karma—none of which was the case. Azucena, as might be expected, had refused. It was contrary to the ethics of her profession to do that sort of thing. But now Azucena saw to her surprise that Cuquita had gotten her way and somehow managed to obtain the books. Azucena was intrigued as to how she had done it. Whom had she bribed? Cuquita left her no time to speculate. Running over to Azucena, she snatched the VRB out of her hands, and quickly stuffed it back in the bag. As she did so, she asked Azucena, in a tone of direct challenge:

"Well, are you going to perpetrate me?"

"What?"

"To the police! Don't even think of it, I'm warning you! Because when it comes to defending my family, I'm capable of anything."

"Oh, don't worry, I won't go to the police. . . . But listen, could you tell me if they also have compact discs where you bought those VRBs?"

Cuquita was amazed by Azucena's sudden interest.

Azucena seemed more bent on taking advantage of Cuquita's connections than on denouncing them. The urgency in her eyes made that clear, so Cuquita decided on impulse to trust her.

"Well . . . yes. But the thing is, it's dangerous to buy them because, I'm warning you, they're totally explicit."

". . . I don't care if they're illicit, just tell me where to get them, please! There's one I have to find!"

"At the black market in Tepito."

"How do I get there?"

"You've never been?"

"No."

"Well, if you've never gone, it's a bitch to find. I'd take you, but my grandmother is waiting for her supper. We can go tomorrow if you want."

"Thanks, but I'd rather go today."

"Okay, go ahead. When you get to Tepito, just ask around."

"Thanks, Cuquita."

Azucena sprang to her feet and, without even a good-bye to Cuquita, ran to the aerophone booth on the corner to transflash herself to Tepito. In a matter of seconds, Azucena was in the heart of the Lagunilla marketplace. The door of the aerophone booth opened, and she was facing a crush of people pushing and elbowing their way into the booth Azucena was vacating. She struggled against the tide and began wandering through the market. Making her way through throngs of people, she headed straight for the stalls where antiques were sold.

Each of the objects there cast its spell on her, making her wonder who had owned it, and in what place and time. She passed several stalls brimming with tires, cars, vacuum cleaners, computers, and other discarded objects, but could find no compact discs. Finally, in one of the booths she saw a portable sound system. Surely they sold CDs there. She walked over to the stall, but the dealer was busy and couldn't wait on her. He was arguing with a customer who wanted to buy a dentist's chair with all sorts of clamps, syringes, and molds for taking dental impressions. Azucena couldn't understand how anyone would be interested in buying such instruments of torture but, after all, in this world there are all sorts of tastes. She waited a while for the haggling to stop, but the two men were equally obstinate and neither of them wanted to budge. There was a pause when the dealer, bored with the discussion, turned and asked Azucena what he could do for her, but she could not summon the words to respond. She didn't have the nerve to ask out loud where to find black-market compact discs. To avoid looking foolish, she asked instead the price of a beautiful silver serving spoon.

Behind her, she heard a woman's voice saying, "That's my spoon. I had set it aside there to buy." Turning around, Azucena found herself face to face with an attractive, dark-haired woman who was reaching for the spoon Azucena was holding up. Azucena gave it to her immediately and apologized, saying she hadn't realized it was already spoken for. She turned and retreated, feeling deeply frustrated. There was a big difference between knowing there was a black market and dealing with the people who ran it. She hadn't the least idea how to begin, where to go, what to ask. Her status as a Super-Evo without any experience in shady dealings certainly had its drawbacks. Her best bet would be to come back another day and bring Cuquita with her.

As she searched for a way out of the labyrinth of booths Azucena suddenly heard a melody emanating from a stall filled with stereos, radios, and television sets. The first thing she noticed when she got there was a sign reading "Music To Cry To," and, below that, in small print, *"Authorized by the Department of Public Health and Welfare."* Although everything appeared to be strictly legal, Azucena had a feeling she would find what she was looking for here. The music was in fact making her cry. It stirred up a deep nostalgia and with it came a wealth of memories. As she listened, Azucena remembered how it had felt to become a single being with Rodrigo, what it had been like to surpass the barrier of skin and to have four arms and legs and eyes; and twenty fingers and nails with which to tear open the gates to Paradise. As Azucena stood there weeping inconsolably, the antique dealer regarded her with great tenderness. After she dried her tears, the dealer quietly removed the CD and handed it to her.

"How much is it?" she asked.

"Nothing."

"Nothing? But I want to buy it . . ."

The dealer smiled amiably. Azucena felt a current of empathy flow between them.

"No one can sell what isn't his," he replied, "nor receive what she hasn't deserved. Take it, it belongs to you."

"Thank you."

Azucena put the CD safely away in her purse. She could hardly tell the dealer that she also needed a player, because she was sure this strange man, who seemed so oddly familiar, would have offered her one as well, and that would be pushing his generosity too far. Just before Azucena left, the dark-haired woman with the silver spoon walked up to the dealer, greeting him warmly, "How are you, Teo!" The dealer hugged her in return. "My dear Citlali," he exclaimed, "what a pleasure to see you!" Azucena walked away quietly, leaving the pair in animated conversation.

At a stall farther down, she bought a Discman so she could listen to her CD, and then she went directly to the nearest aerophone booth. Impatient as a child with a new toy, she was anxious to get home and listen to the music. But when she arrived at the row of aerophone booths, she nearly lost hope. So many people were crowded there that she thought she'd never get in. Eventually, however, she managed to elbow her way through and reached her goal in record time: a half hour. Her feeling of good fortune vanished, however, when she was shoved aside by a man with a large mustache, who forced his way into the booth before her. Infuriated by this latest injustice, her face transformed by rage, Azucena grabbed the man's arm and yanked him back out. He was sweating profusely, and seemed desperate as he pleaded with her.

"Lady! Please let me use the booth!"

"No, you listen to me! It's my turn. I waited just the same as you to get here."

"How long can it hold you up to let me go first? It'll only take me thirty seconds to free up the booth."

People behind them began whistling and shouting, and some of them tried squeezing past the two into the booth. Just then the mustached man saw the adjoining booth had been vacated, and like any sharp transcommuter, dashed inside. Before anyone else could push ahead of her, Azucena claimed her own booth and the matter was resolved.

What a nightmare! It was hard to believe that in the twenty-third century a human being could act like such a beast, especially when one considered the great strides that had been made in the field of science. As she keyed in her aerophone number, Azucena thought of all the benefits she enjoyed as a result of technological advances. To disintegrate, to travel through space and be reintegrated in the blink of an eye. What marvels!

The aerophone door opened and Azucena was about to step into her apartment, but couldn't, because the electromagnetic barrier was preventing her. As the alarm began to sound, she suddenly realized that this was not her own place but, rather, somebody else's, and a couple was passionately making love there. Well, come to think of it, technological advances in Mexico were not so reliable after all. These kinds of mishaps frequently occurred when aerophone lines were crossed or damaged. Although fortunately in such cases there was no danger of being killed, that did not make the incidents any less uncomfortable or annoying.

When the lovers heard the alarm, they abruptly suspended their amorous activities. The woman cried, "It's my husband!" while frantically pulling down her skirt. Azucena did not know what to do or where to look. Her eyes roamed around the room, finally fixing on a photograph on the far wall. Her voice caught in her throat. The mustached man in the photo was none other than the one she had fought with a few moments earlier. No wonder the poor man had been in such a hurry to get home!

Azucena surmised that he must have keyed in his aerophone number before she had jerked him from the booth, and that was why she ended up at his apartment. Desperately, she keyed in her own aerophone number. She had never been in such an embarrassing situation. Before she left, she attempted an apology.

"Sorry, wrong number!"

"Let's see if you can get it right, stupid!"

The aerophone door then closed and reopened a few seconds later. Azucena breathed a sigh of relief to find herself in her own apartment. Or rather, what was left of it. The living room had been ransacked. Furniture and clothing had been tossed in all directions, and right in the middle of the whole mess was the man with the mustache, dead! Blood streamed from his ears. This was what happened to anyone who ignored the sound of the alarm and broke through the protective magnetic field of a house that wasn't his own: the cells of the body would not reintegrate properly, and an excess of pressure would burst the arteries. The poor guy. So the aerophone lines really had been crossed, and in the man's frenzy to catch his wife in the act, he must have dashed out of the booth, without even hearing the alarm. But . . . wait! Azucena hadn't turned the alarm on, for she still had hoped Rodrigo would return and didn't want him to have any problem getting in. So then what *had* happened? And why had her apartment been ransacked?

The first thing she did was to go check the registry box of her building's protection system. There she discovered that someone clearly had tampered with it. The wires had been crossed, and badly reconnected. That meant that someone had intended to kill her. It was only through the ineptitude of the Aerophone Company that her life had been saved. The accidental crossing of the two lines from the aerophone booths had caused this man to die in her place. That was fate for you: she owed her life to incompetence. But now she had new questions. Why had someone wanted to kill her? And who? She had no idea. The only thing she was sure of was that anyone wishing to adjust the master control of the building needed a work permit, and that Cuquita was the only person who could grant them access.

Azucena knocked at Cuquita's door. She had to wait a minute before Cuquita opened up, her eyes filled with tears. Azucena regretted having intruded at the wrong moment. That drunken husband of hers had better not be beating her up again, she thought.

"Good evening, Cuquita."

"Evening."

"Is something wrong?"

"No, I'm just watching *The Right to Live*."

Azucena had totally forgotten Cuquita never did anything while her favorite soap was on.

"I'm sorry, it slipped my mind completely. I just wanted to ask who came to repair my aerophone . . ."

"Who do you think? The men from the Aerophone Company."

"Do you remember if they had a work order?"

"Of course! I don't let just anybody waltz in here."

"Did they mention if they'd be back?"

"Yes, they said they had to finish up tomorrow. So if you don't have any more questions, I'd like to get back to my show . . ."

"Of course, Cuquita. I'm sorry to bother you. See you tomorrow."

"Hmmmpf!"

The sound of Cuquita's door slamming shut in her face stunned Azucena with the same impact as the word "Danger!" ringing in her head. The supposed aerophone workmen would suppose she was dead, and would expect to collect her corpse the next day, supposedly without any problem. Supposing sons of bitches! Coming back tomorrow, but what time? Cuquita hadn't said, but if she knocked at that door again, Cuquita would be the one to kill her. Most likely they'd come by during regular working hours, since they were passing themselves off as repairmen from the Aerophone Company. That meant Azucena still had all night to organize her thoughts and devise a defense strategy. But right now, what she had to do was get rid of the man with the mustache.

Azucena hurried back to her apartment and searched the cuckold's pants pockets for his ID card. Then she keyed in the aerophone number on the card, dragged the man into the booth, and sent him home. It was safe to assume two things: that this had not been the man's lucky day, and that it was turning out to be a day of unpleasant surprises for his wife as well. Azucena could just imagine her face when she saw her husband's corpse. But she didn't want to think about the guilt the woman would suffer later on. Azucena had to remind herself not to get mixed up in other people's affairs. It was an occupational reflex of hers to be always worrying about the traumatic effects of any tragedy upon people.

She felt very sorry for the man who had exchanged fates with her. She would be forever grateful to him. After all, he had saved her from certain death. But who was going to save her now from the dangers she still faced? If only the man had exchanged bodies with her as well, the favor would have been complete, because then the workmen would arrive, find a lifeless body, and take Azucena for dead, thus allowing her to keep on looking for Rodrigo, even if she was in the body of a mustached stranger. Changing bodies . . . that was it! All she had to do was show up early the next morning at the Consumer Protection Agency and she'd be sure to bump into the *coyote* who dealt in soul transplants to unregistered bodies. She knew that this would mean crossing the line into illegal territory, thereby running the risk that the Office of Astral Ascension would find out and cancel her authorization to live with her twin soul. But Azucena could see no other way out. She was ready to try anything.

While on the lookout for the *coyote* the next morning, Azucena joined the line of people waiting for the Consumer Protection offices to open. She couldn't stop thinking about who might want to kill her, and why. She had already worked off her bad karma; she didn't have any enemies, and hadn't committed any crimes. The only person who seemed to hate her was Cuquita, but Azucena didn't think her capable of plotting such a convoluted murder. If she had meant to kill Azucena, she would have buried a kitchen knife in her back long ago. Then who could it be? The ugly sight of the *coyote* rounding the corner interrupted her thoughts. Azucena walked over to meet him. As soon as he saw her approaching, he smiled maliciously.

"So? Changed your mind?"

"Yes."

"Follow me."

Azucena followed him for several blocks as gradually they made their way into the oldest, most run-down part of town. After entering what appeared to be a clothing factory they descended a hidden stairway to the cellar. Azucena was terrified to find herself in the midst of the black-market body trade.

This business owed its inadvertent beginnings to a group of late-twentieth-century scientists who had been experimenting with the artificial insemination of barren women. The procedure worked in the following manner: first an operation was performed to remove an egg from the woman. This egg was then fertilized with the husband's sperm in a test tube. When this test-tube fetus was several weeks old, it was implanted in the woman's womb. Sometimes the woman's body rejected the fetus and spontaneous abortion occurred, in which case the entire process had to be repeated. As the surgical procedure was uncomfortable, the scientists decided that instead of extracting one egg at a time, they would extract several. They would then fertilize them all, so that if for some reason the first attempt at insemination failed, they would have a replacement fetus from the same mother and father ready to be introduced into the uterus. As it was not always necessary to utilize a second fetus, much less a third, the extras were frozen, thus creating the first fetus bank. The fetuses were used for all manner of inhuman experiments up until the time of the Great Earthquake, when the laboratory and fetus bank were buried beneath the rubble. It was not until this century, during the process of remodeling a store, that the frozen fetuses had been discovered. An unscrupulous scientist had immediately purchased them, and with modern techniques succeeded in developing each fetus into an adult body. It seemed an ideal venture. The only person capable of implanting a soul in a human body is the mother. These bodies had no mother and, therefore, possessed no soul. Nor had they ever been registered, for they had not been born at any institution regulated by the government. In other words, they were merely awaiting a transplanted soul in order to exist. And the *coyote* relished playing his part in these good works.

Azucena followed him through the gloomy corridors, not knowing which body to choose. They came in every size, color, and scent. She stopped in front of the body of a woman with beautiful legs. Azucena had always dreamed of having a great pair of legs. Her own were rather spindly, and though she had any number of intellectual and spiritual virtues to compensate for this defect, she had always yearned for shapely legs. Hesitating a moment, but realizing she had no time to waste since the aerophone workmen would soon arrive at her house, she pointed quickly to the woman's body, saying, "That one!" Her choice now made, she requested an immediate transplant. This raised the price, but what could she do? Some things in life you just don't quibble over.

In a matter of seconds, Azucena was installed in the body of a blonde woman with blue eyes and to-die-for legs. She felt very strange, but didn't have time to reflect on her new state. She paid for the transplant and, without even a moment to say good-bye to her old body, was led to a secret aerophone booth from which her old body was transflashed to her apartment. Immediately after, she transflashed to the aerophone booth nearest her home. She wanted to arrive at approximately the same time as her body, because she needed to be there to see the faces of her enemies when they came to pick up her corpse. She had been careful to leave the wires connected just as she had found them. That way, as her old body crossed through the barrier, it would "die," just as her assassins had expected, and they wouldn't bother her anymore.

Standing on the corner near her house, Azucena could observe everything going on in the vicinity of her building. However, she too was being observed, the object of constant whistles and remarks about her legs. How could it be that humanity had evolved so little through all the millennia? Why was it still possible for a pair of shapely legs to derange seemingly rational men? She was the same person she'd been the day before: she felt exactly the same, thought exactly the same, and yet yesterday no one had given her a second look. Who knew how much more time would go by before men rhapsodized over the brilliance of a woman's aura?

Azucena only knew that if she stood on that corner much longer she'd be propositioned outright. She decided to repair to the small café across the street where she could continue her observations while treating herself to one of their delicious sandwiches. Suddenly she felt ravenous. Perhaps it was due to anxiety, perhaps to this new body that needed nourishment, but the fact was, she was dying for a sandwich.

As soon as she entered the café, she was annoyed to find that all the men's eyes were drawn to her. She made her way swiftly among the tables, taking a seat by the window so she could see what was happening outside. As soon as her legs were hidden from view, the café resumed its routine. Most of its regulars were workers from the Moon, who had to begin their commute long before the first newscast of the day. This café provided them not only breakfast, but also an easy way of keeping up with the world. The owners had an ancient television there, as opposed to a Televirtual. This was always a great relief, but especially so in these convulsive times when there had been nothing on the news but replays of Mr. Bush's assassination. Whenever you were watching Televirtual you necessarily found yourself in the middle of the crime scene over and over again, hearing the shot ring out, seeing the bullet enter and then exit the candidate's head carrying part of his brain along with it, seeing Mr. Bush collapse, hearing the screams and confusion, reliving the horror. Most restaurants had their Televirtuals on all day long at the request of a frightened populace who wanted to know what was happening minute by minute. Azucena didn't know how people could stand it, or how they could eat amid all the blood, pain, and smell of gunpowder. At least here, where the owners had refused to install a Televirtual, the customers could make their own decisions about whether or not to watch. Azucena had plenty of reasons for feeling sad and anxious without having to relive all this other suffering.

She decided to concentrate instead on what was happening across the street, while her fellow diners stared blankly at the screen. The broadcast had nothing new to say about Mr. Bush's assassination.

"Police continue to search for evidence at the scene of the crime . . ."

"This cowardly act has jolted the conscience of the world . . ."

"The Planetary Attorney General has issued instructions to all police bureaus to coordinate efforts in locating the assassin . . ."

"The Planetary President condemns this affront to peace and democracy, and promises citizens that every effort is being made to determine as swiftly as possible the motivation for this reprehensible act, as well as the identity of the masterminds behind it . . ."

Azucena listened to the frightened whispering of the other customers. Everyone seemed extremely alarmed, but as soon as the sportscast came on they came to life again. The soccer championships made them forget that there had been any assassination, and their greatest concern became whether or not the young athlete who was the incarnation of Hugo Sánchez would be playing. As far as Azucena could see, the assassin or assassins had planned everything to coincide with the Interplanetary Soccer Championship. Amazing how soccer could distract an entire populace!

Now the Governor of the Federal District was being interviewed, warning people that no rowdy celebrations would be allowed at the Angel de la Independencia monument. For the Earth–Venus match, they planned to disintegrate the monument for an entire week in order to avoid disturbances. Loud protests erupted from the diners at that announcement. Between their whistling and catcalls, it was almost impossible to hear the interview Abel Zabludowsky was conducting from the home of Isabel González, the new candidate for Planetary President, who was bragging about the Nobel Prize she had received in her twentieth-century incarnation as Mother Teresa.

At the end of the interview, the camera focused on an obese young woman whose image filled the screen. Everyone asked who this fat girl was, but no one found out because the interview was abruptly cut off. The only person who didn't seem to mind was Azucena. She was watching the Aerophone Company's spacecraft, which had just landed in front of her building. Two men were emerging from it, but just as they turned and she prepared to scrutinize their faces, her neighbor Julito's spaceship, the *Interplanetary Cockfight*, landed, obstructing her view. Azucena was frantic. Why did he have to land now? One by one, a group of mariachis who provided accompaniment for Julito's cockfights descended from the spacecraft. Their enormous sombreros blocked everything from view.

Azucena quickly paid her bill and ran outside. All she could do now was move closer to the building so she'd be able to see the murderers as they came out, even at the risk of being recognized. But no—how stupid could she be? They couldn't recognize her: she was in a different body. Azucena laughed at herself. She had changed bodies so fast that her mind hadn't taken it in.

Azucena sat on the stairs outside her building to wait. Minutes later, she saw the aerophone workmen coming, accompanied by Cuquita, who was sobbing loudly. They were saying good-bye to her in the doorway, telling her how sorry they were. Azucena remained frozen in place, not so much because her supposed death had moved Cuquita to tears, but because one of these two murderers was none other than the former ballerina in line behind her at the Consumer Protection Agency, the one who had wanted a woman's body so badly. My God! Had they killed her for her body? But if that was the case, why hadn't they taken it with them? Apparently, to continue the pretense. Now Azucena was thoroughly confused, because the spacehearse from the Gayosso Funeral Home would pick up her body and disintegrate it in outer space. So if the men from Gayosso took the body, how would the ex-ballerina get possession of it? Did he have contacts at the funeral home?

Her friend Julito meanwhile was warming up his mariachi group with the song "Sabor a mí." The music interrupted Azucena's train of thought and made her cry. She had been abnormally sensitive to music lately. Music! She really was stupid! In all the confusion, she had forgotten to take the compact disc from her apartment. If she was lucky, the opera that had been playing during her examination for the job at COPE would be on that CD.

Now she was on the right track. She had to get into her apartment, but her new body wasn't registered in the master control. She had to have that CD! So without a second thought she rang Cuquita's doorbell. Cuquita answered on the videophone.

"Yes?"

"Cuquita, it's me. Please let me in."

"What do you mean, 'me'? I don't know you."

"Cuquita, you're not going to believe this, but it's me—Azucena."

"What? Yeah, right!"

With that Cuquita hung up. Her image disappeared from the video screen. Azucena rang again.

"You, again? Look, if you don't leave, I'm calling the police."

"All right, call them. I think they'll be very interested to learn where you bought those VRBs for your grandmother."

Cuquita didn't answer. She was left speechless. Who the hell *was* this woman, and how did she know about those books for the blind? There was only one other person in the world who knew about the VRBs, and that was Azucena.

"Cuquita, please let me in and I'll explain everything. Okay?"

Cuquita finally gave in.

As Azucena told her story, Cuquita began to feel closer to her. She no longer looked on Azucena as an enemy, nor as some superior creature to be envied. For the first time, she saw Azucena as someone she could be friends with, even though Azucena belonged to the political party of the Evos, who were highly evolved. The class conflict between them had always been a great barrier, and had been recently intensified due to a new government regulation stating that all Evos should display a visible sign on their aura: a six-pointed star at forehead level. The purpose was the immediate identification of Evos, so that they would be given preferential treatment wherever they went. Evos enjoyed a wide variety of advantages, including the best accommodations in spaceships, hotels, and resorts. More important, only they were eligible to fill positions of trust. That was only logical; after all, it would never occur to anybody to place the nation's resources in the hands of a Non-Evo. On the contrary, it was almost a given that because of their criminal past and their lack of spiritual enlightenment, they would inevitably loot the nation's coffers.

To Cuquita, this situation was highly unjust. How were the Non-Evos ever going to be able to work their way out of their low spiritual rating if no one gave them the chance to demonstrate they were evolving? It wasn't fair that just because they had raised a little hell in one life, they were branded as riffraff in this one. They had to fight for the right to exercise their free will, and this was why the Party for the Retribution of Inequities had been founded.

Cuquita was an enthusiastic party activist, and her greatest aspiration was to win the right to meet her twin soul, just like her Evo neighbor had done. How she had envied Azucena on that day when she found out she and Rodrigo had met! But just look how fate could play out. Here they were, both in the same boat: anxious, abandoned, and desperate.

Cuquita's expression softened now, and she was moved to tears as Azucena shared her love story with her. The two women hugged each other like old friends and promised to keep each other's secrets. Cuquita would not reveal any information about Azucena's true identity, and Azucena would not tell anyone about the VRBs Cuquita had bought for her grandmother.

And now that they were beginning to trust each other, Cuquita allowed herself to ask Azucena a question: what was Azucena going to do on Monday when she was supposed to turn in her papers at COPE, because the aurograph they'd taken of her wouldn't correspond to her new body? Azucena's jaw dropped. She'd never thought of that. When you focus on pure survival, you're bound to lose overall perspective. How was she going to handle this? Then she remembered that they had closed the window before she handed in her papers. This would allow her to have an aurograph of her new body taken somewhere to substitute for the one taken at COPE and . . . Suddenly all the color drained from Azucena's face. She had a new body! When she had had her soul transplant, she hadn't considered that the microcomputer would be left behind in her old body. Now there was a *real* problem. Without that microcomputer she couldn't go anywhere near COPE, because they photographed the thoughts of everyone within a block's radius of the building. She'd have to find Dr. Díez right away so that he could install another microcomputer in her head.

Azucena took a deep breath before knocking at the door of Dr. Díez's consulting room. She had had to climb up the fifteen floors because the Doctor's aerophone kept ringing busy. It must have been out of order. And since she could not use the aerophone in her own office because her new body wasn't registered in its electromagnetic protective field, she had made the climb on foot. When she had more or less recovered her breath, she knocked at her good friend's door. It was slightly ajar. Azucena pushed it and discovered instantly why Dr. Díez's line kept ringing busy: because as the doctor had died, his body had fallen right across the doorway of the aerophone booth, obstructing the mechanism that closed it. The doctor had perished in the same way as the mustached stranger.

Azucena felt she couldn't breathe. What was going on? A second crime in less than a week. She began to shake. And that was when she heard Dr. Díez's African violet quietly weeping. Dr. Díez had the same habit as Azucena of leaving his plants connected to the Plantspeaker. Azucena felt sick and ran into the bathroom to vomit. She had to get out of the building. She fled from the office, taking the African violet with her. If she left it behind, it would die of grief.

Azucena was lying on her bed. She felt lonely, so very lonely. Sadness does not make good company; it numbs the soul. Azucena turned on the Televirtual, more to feel someone next to her than to watch any particular program. Immediately, Abel Zabludowsky appeared at her side. Azucena snuggled next to him. As a Televirtual image, Abel did not feel Azucena's presence, since he was not really there but in the Televirtual broadcasting studio. The body in Azucena's bedroom was an illusion, a chimera, but still it made Azucena feel that she was not alone.

Abel was discussing the long career of the former candidate for Planetary President. Mr. Bush had been a man of color born into one of the most prominent families in the Bronx. He had spent his early life there, attending the best schools. Since childhood he had shown a natural inclination for public service, performing countless humanitarian acts, and so on and so on. But Azucena heard none of it. She didn't care what Abel was saying at the moment. All she wanted to know was who had killed Dr. Díez, and why. His death affected her deeply, not only because he was a good friend, but also because without his help she'd never be able to work at COPE, and that meant the end of any hope of finding Rodrigo.

Oh, Rodrigo! How long ago it seemed that she had shared this bed with him. Now she was lying there with Abel Zabludowsky, who was only a pathetic and illusory substitute. Rodrigo was so different. He had the most profound eyes she had ever known, the most protective arms, the most delicate touch, the firmest, most sensual muscles. During the time she had spent in his arms, she had felt protected, loved, alive! Desire flooded every cell in her body, her blood hammered at her temples in passion, warmth invaded her body just as it had . . . just as it was doing right now— in Abel Zabludowsky's arms! Azucena opened her eyes in alarm. Could she really be such a horny bitch? What was going on? The incredible answer to that question was that she was cuddled against *Rodrigo's* body; Abel Zabludowsky had disappeared. Only his voice could be heard alerting the public:

"The man you are now viewing is the alleged accomplice of Mr. Bush's assassin and is being sought by the police."

An aerophone number appeared on the screen so that anyone who might have seen the suspect could immediately contact the Planetary Prosecutor General's office. Azucena leapt up. Impossible! That was a lie, a filthy lie! Rodrigo had been with her on the day of the assassination. He had had nothing to do with that crime. Even so, she was grateful they had confused Rodrigo with the accused criminal, because it had allowed her to be with him. Gently, she began caressing his body, but her pleasure was short-lived.

For the beloved image of Rodrigo slowly faded, to be replaced by that of her companion from the line at the Consumer Protection Agency. It appeared that the frustrated former ballerina who had intended to kill her had also murdered Dr. Díez.

What was going on? Who was this man? What was he after? Was he a psychopath? Abel Zabludowsky's voice was now answering those very questions, explaining that this was in fact the man who had assassinated Mr. Bush. Aurographic tests had proved it. He had been found dead at his home from an overdose of pills. Why had he committed suicide? And now, who would be able to prove that Rodrigo had had nothing to do with the murder? Azucena had too many questions to deal with at once. What she needed was answers, urgently. The only one who could give them to her, however, was Anacreonte. She was sorely tempted to reestablish communication with him, but her pride got in the way. She wasn't going to reach out to him, only to have her arm twisted. She had told him she could manage her own life, and that was exactly what she was going to do, whatever the cost.

CD
Track 3

Zongo took a crack at Borondongo,
Borondongo then whacked Bernabé
Bernabé started beating Muchilanga
Who, kicking Burundanga,
Got two swollen feet.

Why did Zongo take a crack at Borondongo?
'Cause Borondongo took a whack at Bernabé.

Why did Borondongo take a whack at Bernabé?
'Cause Bernabé started beating Muchilanga.

Why did Bernabé try to beat Muchilanga?
'Cause Muchilanga kicked Burundanga.

Why did Muchilanga kick Burundanga?
'Cause Burundanga got him two swollen feet.

O. BOUFFARTIQUE

8

That Azucena is stubborn as a mule. Ever since she stopped speaking to me, and got it into her head to act on her own, all she's done is screw things up. It's exasperating to watch her do one stupid thing after another, and not be able to intervene. I've said it before: that little brat is used to getting her own blessed way. I've had it!

And the worst of it is that when she goes into a depression, no one can snap her out of it. I've been monitoring her insomnia for a while. She couldn't sleep because, among other things, her new body doesn't fit in the hollow her old one left in the mattress. So she ended up sitting on the edge of the bed for a long time. Then she cried for about twenty minutes. And blew her nose fifteen times while she was at it. Then she stared at the ceiling for thirty minutes. After that, she studied herself in the mirror of the antique armoire facing her bed. She slipped her hand beneath her night-gown and stroked herself, slowly, very slowly. Then, perhaps to take absolute possession of her new body, she masturbated. Then she cried again for another twenty minutes. Next she compulsively wolfed down four sopes, three tamales, and five custard-filled cornucopias. Ten minutes later, she vomited everything she'd eaten, soiling her nightgown. She took it off. And washed it. And hung it up to dry. Next, she took a shower. And, as she shampooed her head, she ached for the long hair she used to have. Then she went back to bed, where she tossed and turned like a top.

She's been lying there in a catatonic haze for five hours. But at no time, not one single instant, has it occurred to her to listen to my advice. If only she'd let me talk to her, I'd tell her that the first thing she has to do is listen to the compact disc; that's her ticket to the past. That's where she'll find the key to everything, but she hasn't done that because she feels she's not in the mood to cry! Talk about depression!

No question about it: waiting does erode hope. Azucena is waiting for Rodrigo to come back. I'm waiting for her to find a way out of the state she's in. Pavana, Rodrigo's Guardian Angel, is waiting for me to work with her. My sweetheart Lilith is waiting for me to complete Azucena's education so we can go away on vacation. We're all spinning our wheels because of her stupidity!

She doesn't understand that everything that happens in this world happens for a reason, and not just randomly. One act, however minimal, unleashes a chain reaction in the world around us. Creation has a perfect operating mechanism, but to run smoothly it requires that each being who is a part of it carry out his or her appointed role correctly. If we don't, the rhythm of the entire Universe is disrupted. It is impossible, therefore, for Azucena even to consider acting on her own! For even the smallest particle of an atom knows it must receive orders from above; that it cannot make its own decisions. If one of the cells in the body were to decide it was guide and mistress of its destiny, and opt to do whatever its whim might be, it would become a cancer that would completely alter the healthy functioning of the organism. When one forgets one is a part of the whole, that one bears the Divine Essence within; when one ignores the fact one is connected with the Cosmos—like it or not—one ends up foolishly lying in bed dwelling on sheer nonsense.

Azucena is not isolated, as she believes she is. Nor is she disconnected, as she imagines. Damn, how can she be so stupid! She thinks she has nothing. She doesn't realize that this Nothing that surrounds her is sustaining her, and will always sustain her wherever she is; this Nothing will keep her in harmony wherever she may go; this Nothing will always choose the proper moment to communicate with her, so that she can hear its message. Every cell of the human body bears a message, sent from the brain. And where does the brain get it? From the human being in command of that body. And where did that human being get the message? Her Guardian Angel dictated it to her, and so on. There is a Supreme Intelligence that directs us to foster the balance between creation and destruction. Activity and rest regulate the battle between these two forces. The force of creation imposes order on chaos. Then comes the period of rest before a new effort required to control disorder. If this rest is overly prolonged, creation is endangered, for destruction, sensing that creation has lost its force, springs into action again. It's as if a plant that had grown in sunlight were suddenly placed in the shade; it is deprived of the strength to sustain itself, and so the destructive force sees to its death. That is precisely the danger Azucena finds herself in as a result of her paralysis.

One person's inaction paralyzes the world. The rhythm of the Universe is broken. If one day the moon stopped still in its orbit, a catastrophe would result. If one day the clouds went on strike and refused to rain, a widespread drought would follow. The drought would cause famine, and a severe enough famine, the end of the human race. The greater the paralysis, the greater the depression, and the greater the depression, the greater the calamities to follow.

Sometimes a person seems to be paralyzed but really isn't; she is merely rearranging things inside, which eventually will put her in harmony with the Cosmos. The real problem arrives when total paralysis occurs. Precisely what Azucena is suffering. It's not so bad that she is doing nothing about it outwardly; what's bad is that she's doing nothing about it inwardly. Not only does she not want to listen to me; she does not want to listen to herself. And since she's not allowing herself to hear her inner voice, she doesn't know what action she should take. She doesn't get the message because her mind isn't allowing it in. She's keeping it filled with negative thoughts. She's going to have to let them out, because they're jamming her line of communication.

The Supreme Intelligence uses a direct line, which, if it encounters interference, veers off in a different direction, with the result that its message either is heard only faintly or is misinterpreted. The solution for this problem is a spiritual alignment. This kind of alignment has nothing to do with the kind that operates on Earth. The latter is like a pyramid in which those at the bottom do what those on top command, and nothing else; and that's when human beings lose responsibility for their actions and submit to what others tell them. No, that is to append, not align, oneself.

The kind of alignment I'm talking about consists of getting oneself in syntony with the loving energy circulating throughout the Cosmos. This is achieved by relaxing and letting life flow among all the cells of the body. Then Love, the cosmic DNA, will remember its genetic message, its origins, the mission assigned it. That mission is unique and personal—not collective, as is avowed in one kind of earthly alignment. The moment Azucena can do that, her entire being will breathe cosmic energy, and will remember it is not alone—much less, without Love.

It isn't so easy to understand Love. Usually people think they find it through a partner. But the love we experience while making love with another is only a pale reflection of what is truly Love. One's partner is only the intermediary through whom we receive Divine Love. Through the kiss, the embrace, the soul receives all the peace necessary to align itself and make the connection with Divine Love. But be warned: that does not mean that our partner possesses that Love, nor is he or she the only one who can bestow it. Nor is it true that if that person leaves, he will take Love with him, leaving us unprotected. Divine Love is infinite. It is everywhere and entirely within reach at every moment. It is foolish of Azucena to limit it to the small space of Rodrigo's arms. If she only realized that all she has to do is learn to open her consciousness to energy on other planes to receive the Love she needs in full store. If she only realized that at this very moment she is surrounded by Love, that it is circulating about her, despite the fact no one is kissing or caressing or embracing her. If she only realized that she is a beloved daughter of the Universe, she would no longer feel lost.

Azucena blames me for everything that is happening to her; she fails to realize that losing Rodrigo is something she had to go through, because the moment she throws herself into the search she will find, in the process, the solution to a problem that has been plaguing humanity for thousands of years. That is the real reason behind all the doubts she is experiencing.

There is a problem of cosmic origin affecting all inhabitants of the planet, and she is the one charged with resolving it. Although it is a mission that actually involves every one of us, Azucena's ego has minimized and converted it into a question of a personal nature. Her bruised and battered self-esteem makes her believe that the whole world is against her, and that everything that is happening affects her alone. But she is a part of this world, and anything that affects her also affects the world. And the world has much more important things to think about than destroying Azucena. That would be absurd, anyway, because in destroying a human being it would be destroying itself, and the Universe has no inclination toward self-destruction.

If only she could be here beside me in space! She would see her past and her future at the same time, and thus understand why I allowed Rodrigo to disappear. If only she could see that all her possibilities did not die with Dr. Díez. If only she could see that she has much better alternatives at hand than those the doctor offered her. If only she would exercise her free will in the right way. Hell, it isn't that difficult to do! Life will never place us at a crossroads where one way leads to perdition. It places us only in circumstances we are able to handle. What usually happens is that people allow themselves to be defeated by circumstances that they perceive as insurmountable obstacles—but nothing could be farther from the truth.

The Universe will place us in situations that correspond to our degree of evolution. That's why in Azucena's particular case, I always opposed rushing her meeting with Rodrigo. Not because she wasn't sufficiently evolved, and not because Rodrigo still had outstanding debts, but because Azucena needed to learn to exercise more control over her impulsiveness and rebelliousness before confronting her present situation. I knew very well that she was going to fly off the handle, and I certainly got that part right! Her confused state of mind prevents her from seeing the truth.

On Earth, truth always exists amid confusion and lies. Confusion comes from our taking as truth things that are not. Truth never is found outside oneself. Each of us has the capacity, if we communicate with ourselves, to find truth. It is only logical that Azucena is confused at this moment, for externally she has encountered nothing but chaos, lies, murder, fear, and indecision. She believes that truth is solid as a rock, but that is not the case. In the face of the general despair that characterizes the outside world, she should be able to say: I don't have to participate in this chaos, even though I realize it is all around me, because I AM NOT CHAOS. At the moment she denies as truth the reality surrounding her, she will find her own truth, and with it, peace. Since what is internal becomes external, individual peace will lead to universal peace. But since Azucena is in no condition to recognize this at the moment, I must arrange for her to be able to help someone else. By helping another, she will be helping herself.

9

Azucena was startled out of bed by a series of loud knocks at the door. She opened it to find Cuquita, Cuquita's grandmother, Cuquita's suitcases, and Cuquita's parrot staring her in the face. The parrot looked well enough, but Cuquita and her grandmother were all black and blue.

Azucena didn't know what to say; she could only ask them in. Cuquita then proceeded to explain her problems. Her husband was beating her more each day. She couldn't take any more. But the last straw was that today he had beat up her grandmother, and that was something she wouldn't stand for. She asked Azucena if they could stay a few days with her. Azucena said that would be all right. What else could she do? Cuquita knew about the body exchange and Azucena didn't want her to inform the authorities. Of course, she could do the same thing, report how Cuquita had illegally obtained the VRBs, but she didn't want to do that. She had much more to lose than Cuquita. So Azucena decided to put her misery aside and share her apartment with them. After all, it would only be for a few days.

As soon as Cuquita took over the kitchen, Azucena began to feel she'd been invaded. True, the grandmother urgently needed a linden-flower tea to calm her down, but what annoyed Azucena was that Cuquita hung the parrot's cage right over the breakfast table. No one could see past it, and besides, that meant from now on they'd all be eating with bird feathers up their nostrils.

Her sense of being displaced was intensified when Cuquita installed her grandmother on the living room sofa bed. The old woman was very docile and quiet, but still she was in the way. Now every time Azucena went to the kitchen for a glass of water, she had to climb over her. But the crowning blow came when Cuquita took over Azucena's bedroom. She dropped her things everywhere. Azucena followed behind, trying to reestablish order. For example, she suggested in a friendly way that Cuquita might keep her suitcase of Avon samples in the closet. Azucena did not want to think how Rodrigo would react the day he returned and found the damn thing in the middle of the bedroom. But Cuquita categorically refused, saying she had to give a demonstration the next day and the only way she'd remember was if she kept it out.

Azucena could scarcely believe her eyes. Cuquita was the proud owner of a stupefying collection of horrible, tasteless bric-a-brac. Most outrageous was a strange apparatus that resembled a primitive typewriter. Cuquita handled it with special care. When Azucena asked her what it was, Cuquita replied with great pride:

"One of my inventions."

"Oh? It is? What does it do?"

"It's a cybernetic Ouija."

Cuquita set the apparatus on the night table, and gave a demonstration as if she were selling an Avon product. The apparatus was put together from an ancient computer, a fax, a Stone Age record player, a telegraph, a scale, and an apothecary flask connected to a strange assortment of tubes, a clay tortilla platter edged with quartz crystals, and a wooden New Year's Eve party clacker. In the center of the platter was the outline of two hands, indicating the position where the subject's hands should be placed.

"Uhhh . . . very . . . striking! What's it for?"

"What do you mean? You never used a Ouija?"

"No."

"Oh yeah, I forgot, you Evos are so high and mighty you don't need any gadgets to get in touch with your Guardian Angels. But we don't have your superiority complexion. No one does anything for us, we have to scratch our own backs. And if we want to find out anything about our past lives, we have to rig up some lousy contraption like this."

Azucena was moved by Cuquita's complaint. You could see a mile away that she was boiling over with resentment and pain. As an astroanalyst, she knew she couldn't let Cuquita's negative emotions keep resonating that way without treatment, so she tried to give her some confidence and buck her up.

"Don't be angry, Cuquita. The reason I asked you what it's for wasn't because I never used a Ouija, but because I'd never seen one that was so . . . uh, complex, so . . . different, so . . . inventive! Show me how it works, will you?" Cuquita, feeling more secure, immediately calmed down and began talking in a less strident tone.

"Oh! Well, you see, it's real simple. If you want to go and communicate with your Guardian Angel, you put your hands here on the platter like this and think your question, and presto, you get your answer back on this facts machine. Now, if you want to talk with loved ones who've already passed on, you fix it so no one can pick up what they say—you know, in case they bring up secret treasures and stuff like that—so what you do is telegraph your question, and you get your answer back right here."

"Wow, that's fantastic!"

Cuquita's face glowed from the feeling that she was appreciated, and there was a flush in her cheeks that competed with her purple bruises.

"Hey, that's not all! Let's say someone wants to sell you something, like a record or some antiquary that might have belonged to, let's say, a famous singer like Pedro Infante, and you want to know if it's the genuine article, or maybe somebody's trying to put one over on you. So, let's say it's a record, right? Well, you'd put it right here," she said, pointing to the record player, "or, if it's some other kind of hairloom, we put it in this thing here," pointing to the flask, "with this special fluid that breaks it down like it was mushed ice, and then this computer prints out its whole history, told by the hairloom itself, and over here on the facts machine out come color pictures of all the people who ever touched it. Or, put it another way, you kill two birds with one, because on the one hand you make sure you're not being sold a pill of goods, and at the same time you're getting a free picture of your favorite star. How's that?"

Azucena was truly dumbfounded. How was it possible that this woman who had never finished elementary school was capable of inventing such a sophisticated apparatus? Of course, it remained to be seen what it could actually do, but, in any case, her initiative was remarkable. Cuquita was beside herself with pleasure when she saw that Azucena was truly interested in her invention.

"Listen, Cuquita. I have only one question. What if I wanted to know, for example, whom a bed had belonged to? How would you find out?"

"Well, you take a splinter from it and we put it in the flask."

"But what if it's a brass bed?"

"Then, hey, don't buy it! Come on, I can't go around thinking of everything. You know what? Maybe we'd better stop right here, because I'm beginning to get paranotic."

Cuquita was starting to heat up, and Azucena wanted to avoid that, especially now that they were sharing an apartment.

"Oh, you haven't told me what that party favor's for."

"Oh, that clacker thing is the most important part. You whirl it around, and the sound it makes changes the energy in the room where you're going to receive shortwave messages. It's to prevent interference from demons."

"I see . . ."

Azucena could not avoid feeling an enormous curiosity about communicating with the beyond. Ever since breaking off with Anacreonte, she had had no idea of what was happening or what was going to happen. This might be her opportunity to find out about Rodrigo without having to submit to Anacreonte.

"Listen, could I ask it a question?"

"Sure, go ahead!"

Cuquita felt greatly flattered by Azucena's request, and immediately began whirling the wooden clacker all around the bedroom. Then she gave Azucena instructions about how to place her hands on the platter and how to concentrate when she asked her question. Azucena followed Cuquita's instructions to the letter, and, in a few seconds, the fax began printing out a reply: *My dear child, you are going to see him much sooner than you think.*

Azucena's eyes filled with tears. Cuquita put an arm around her protectively.

"You see? It's all going to work out."

Azucena nodded. She could not find words, she was so happy. And Cuquita felt completely vindicated. This was the first time anyone had used her invention, and now she knew that it worked. The atmosphere in the house immediately felt different. Azucena realized that the small attention she had given Cuquita was paying substantial rewards. She began to see the brighter side of her present circumstances. After all, it could be very entertaining and beneficial to have Cuquita with her for a few days. The news that she would soon be seeing Rodrigo had so greatly improved her spirits that it drove all the black clouds from her head. For the first time in many days, her heart was not oppressed. She thought that this might be a good moment to listen to her CD. Once she relaxed, she realized how tired she was. She suggested to Cuquita that they turn in, and Cuquita agreed. It was three o'clock in the morning, and it had been a long day. Azucena put on her headphones, lay down on her side of the bed, and closed her eyes.

While Cuquita was making her own preparations for bed, she suddenly spied the remote control of the Televirtual. She felt a surge of pleasure and forgot about her exhaustion and her bruises. All her life she had longed for a Televirtual, but had never had the money to buy one. The closest she had come was a run-of-the-mill 3-D set. Cuquita sat down on her side of the bed, pressed the ON button, and started cruising the channels like a five-year-old. Azucena didn't even notice. She was quietly listening to her CD with her eyes closed.

Cuquita, like any worthy representative of the party of the Non-Evos, was lapping up the talk show *Cristina* with morbid pleasure. That night they were broadcasting live from a penal planet prison. Through the device of a photomental camera, the thoughts of the worst criminals were being converted into virtual-reality images. Televirtual viewers were transported to bedrooms where incest, rapes, and murders had occurred. Cuquita was delighted. She hadn't felt such strong emotions since her school days, when the same pedagogical methods had been used to teach students about the horrors of war. Students were set down in the midst of a battle, so they could smell death, so they could feel in the flesh all its pain, anguish, and horror. It was well known that the only way human beings learned anything was by perceiving experiences through the senses. It was hoped that after this direct exposure, no one would dream of starting a war or torturing anyone or committing any kind of illegal act, since they would know how it felt.

It hadn't worked out that way, however. Admittedly, crime had been brought under control, but not so much because people had learned their lesson, as because of advances in technology. Until Mr. Bush's assassination, no one in ages had dared commit a murder. Again, not because they didn't have the desire, but because of their fear of punishment. New devices meant that no one escaped capture. Human beings, then, had no choice but to learn to repress their criminal instincts. That did not mean they didn't have them. Not in the least: witness the sensational ratings of shows like *Cristina, Oprah, Donahue, Sally,* and others, in which the Televirtual audience vicariously experienced all manner of base emotions. The government allowed these shows to be broadcast because they channeled murderous urges, making it easier to keep them under control.

Cuquita couldn't believe how wonderful it was to be in the thick of the action. She felt thrilled to be present at the murder of Sharon Tate. She loved the sensation of fear coursing through her, causing goose bumps, making her hair stand on end, paralyzing her voice. The violence nauseated her, but, like any good masochist, she thought that was part of the fun. Then came the commercials, right in the midst of her sufferings. Cuquita was furious. She frantically began switching channels, searching for a similar program. Suddenly her eyes were caught by a burning red glow: lava had always exercised a hypnotic power over her.

The station was broadcasting live from the planet Korma. Isabel González was walking among the survivors of the eruption, having traveled there with a group bringing disaster relief. She wanted this to be the kickoff for her campaign. Thanks to Televirtual transmission, Cuquita was suddenly in an ideal spot to savor everything: right between Isabel and Abel Zabludowsky, who kept commenting on how incredibly well Isabel carried off her 150 years. "And, why shouldn't she!" thought Cuquita. Isabel had spent years as an interplanetary ambassador. On each journey she had shaved off a large number of years because of the difference in time between planets. When she returned from a voyage that for her had lasted a week, she found that on Earth five years had gone by. But Cuquita wouldn't have traded places with Isabel, even if she did look so young. All she could think of was how many burritos Isabel could have eaten during those lost years. How many New Year's Eve parties she must have missed!

As Isabel began distributing sandwiches among the victims of the eruption, all the primitives rushed toward her to receive their share. Isabel's bodyguards stepped forward to protect her, lashing out indiscriminately.

Cuquita jumped up from the bed and began screaming, "Azucena, Azucena! Look!"

Isabel's two bodyguards turned out to be: one, the supposed Aerophone Company workman, and two . . . Azucena! Well, that is, the once and former Azucena, because a different person was occupying her body now. In a daze, Azucena opened her eyes to see what was going on. She watched as Isabel's guards moved her away from the mob of starving savages. Azucena was stupefied to see that one of the guards had her former body, and that standing beside it was the supposed aerophone repairman. But she nearly fainted as she saw Isabel approach a man sitting apart from the others. *Rodrigo!* Azucena had been dreaming about him when Cuquita awakened her, and now she didn't know whether what she was seeing was still part of her fantasy, or was real.

Rodrigo was painstakingly carving a wooden spoon with a stone. As soon as he saw Isabel approach, he stood up. She offered him a sandwich, but instead of taking it, Rodrigo walked toward Ex-Azucena and stroked her face, trying to place her. Ex-Azucena was getting nervous. Isabel was intrigued. Cuquita was outraged. And Azucena, with all her heart, devoted herself to caressing Rodrigo for a few brief moments. It wasn't much time, but it was long enough to make her despair boundless as she watched him vanish into thin air. The images from Korma were replaced by those of soccer players on a practice field. The news had shifted to the sports segment. Cuquita and Azucena turned to each other. Azucena was weeping hopelessly.

"That was Rodrigo!"

"That man?" Cuquita was shocked at the pathetic state he was in.

"Yes."

"And that was *you!*"

"Yes."

"What's your financé doing on Korma?"

Azucena had no idea. All she knew was that she was in one hell of a mess. If the men who tried to murder her, and who stole her body, were Isabel's private bodyguards, then Isabel had had a hand in all this. If Isabel was involved, then she had a huge advantage: power. And since she had the power, going head to head with her was going to be a real nightmare.

Azucena quickly tried to list reasons why Isabel might have wanted to have her killed. Could Isabel have been behind the assassination of Mr. Bush? But then why had she chosen Rodrigo to be the fall guy? Who knows? Also, she must have found out somehow that Rodrigo had been making love to Azucena the entire night of the crime, so the next logical step was to order the elimination of his alibi, that is, Azucena.

All right, but what would Isabel's next move be? Granted it was expedient for Isabel to have Rodrigo as assassin, but how was she going to keep him from protesting his innocence to the authorities? Maybe it wasn't in her plans for him even to make a statement. Maybe that's why she had him taken to Korma: to leave him there forever. Maybe . . . maybe. What Azucena couldn't understand was how Isabel could risk having everything unravel. What if one of the Televirtual viewers watching the news at that very moment recognized Rodrigo and turned him in? What would happen then? That was the question. Azucena couldn't see any way out of her dilemma, but Cuquita, without the same analytical powers, took the situation in hand immediately.

"We'll just have to go after your fiancé and bring him back."

"We can't, the police are looking for him. They say he's implicated in Mr. Bush's assassination. But it isn't true, he was with me that night."

"I can swear to that, all right. I couldn't sleep for all the squeaking the bed was making."

Azucena thought back to their night of love, and sobbed even louder.

"Don't cry, it doesn't matter that the police are searching for him. We'll just get him a different body, and that'll be the end of the problem. We're not living in my grandmother's times anymore, when they used to say, 'The house is on fire, the children have gone, O woe is me!' No, in times like this you have to put your best face forward. Dry your tears, and to battle!"

Azucena stopped her crying and yielded meekly to Cuquita's guidance. She couldn't take any more. She had received too many blows in too short a time. She had lost her twin soul, had been on the verge of being murdered, had been forced to undergo a soul transplant, had discovered the murder of a close friend, had witnessed her beloved body occupied by an assassin, and, finally, had found Rodrigo but under terrible circumstances, in grave danger and in a place that was for all practical purposes out of her reach. It was more than she could take. She felt profoundly fragile, isolated, drained, incapable of making a decision.

"We'll have to leave first thing tomorrow."

"How can we? I don't have any money. And you have less! And interplanetary flights are so expensive."

"Yeah, they're not exactly bargain basement, but we'll find a way."

Cuquita and Azucena stared at each other for a moment. Then suddenly there was a brilliant spark in Cuquita's eyes, a stroke of inspiration that she transmitted to Azucena. Azucena grasped it instantly, and they both shouted together:

"Good old Julito!"

Azucena was beginning to give up hope. Julito's interplanetary spaceship was more like a milk train, stopping at every planet between Earth and Korma. Every time it landed, Azucena felt as if the Universe had ground to a halt. She had approached Julito to ask about the possibility of a direct flight, but her old pal had flatly refused and, as subtly as possible, had reminded Azucena that she was in no position to demand anything, since she was traveling free. Besides, Julito had to make the stops because, in addition to the *Interplanetary Cockfight*'s routine flights to underevolved planets, he had two sidelines that brought in a major portion of his income: home-delivery grandchildren, and express-mates.

In the most distant space colonies there were elderly men and women who had never been able to marry or have grandchildren and were, as a result, subject to terrible depressions. Julito had been struck with the brilliant idea of renting out grandchildren, and this was his peak season, since vacation time was just beginning at the orphanages. Another of his enterprises much in demand was that of express-delivery husbands and wives. When young adults were assigned special missions for long periods of time on very distant planets, they often suffered inflamed hormones. As it was highly undesirable for them to have sexual relations with the aborigines, their earthmates would often send them a substitute husband or wife to satisfy their appetites. And that wasn't all. At the specific request of the partner, the surrogate lover learned prose passages and poems by memory and recited them in the client's ear while they were making love.

All of which was why the spaceship—besides carrying game cocks, mariachis, starlets, and entertainers for the cockfights—was stuffed with children and surrogate husbands and wives. Azucena thought she was going insane. She needed silence and calm to organize her thoughts, and the chaos that reigned in the ship was just too much for her. Children were running everywhere, the mariachis were practicing "Amorcito corazón" with a singer who was the incarnation of the great Pedro Infante, the surrogate partners were practicing their routines on the starlets, Cuquita's blind grandmother was practicing her crochet, Cuquita's drunken husband was practicing his vomiting, the cocks were practicing their cockadoodledoos—and the *coyote* who had sold Azucena her body was practicing, unsuccessfully, an exchange of souls between a starlet and a rooster.

Given these circumstances, Azucena had only two options: to go completely round the bend, crazed by the chaos, or to give in and practice something herself. She decided to rehearse the kiss she was going to give Rodrigo the minute she saw him. So with great eagerness, placing her index finger between her lips, she practiced again and again the best sensations she could evoke with a succulent kiss. She stopped, however, when one of the surrogates offered to rehearse with her. She was embarrassed to have been

118

discovered, and concluded that she'd better keep her distance from all the crazies on board.

Like all lovers throughout the ages, Azucena wanted to be alone, to be able to think about Rodrigo with more serenity. She was distracted and annoyed by the company of her fellow passengers. Since she couldn't make them vanish from the ship, she closed her eyes to retreat into her memories. She needed to reconstruct her image of Rodrigo, to give him shape, to remember the magic of being one with her twin soul, to relive those sensations of self-sufficiency, fullness, boundlessness. Only Rodrigo's presence could give meaning to her reality, only the light that illuminated his smile could free her from the sadness withering her soul. The idea that she would soon see him gave her new life.

She put on her earphones and began to listen to the compact disc. All she wanted was to be in a world different from the one in which she was living. She had already lost hope that the music would trigger a regression to the life she had lived with Rodrigo in the past. The night before, she had listened all the way through, hoping to hear the music she had heard while taking her examination at COPE, but nothing. Now that she knew in advance that the music on this CD was not what she was looking for, she was able to relax and lose herself in the melody. Oddly enough, it was in relinquishing her obsession about having a regression that she was able to let the music flow freely into her subconscious. Easily, spontaneously, she was borne to the former life she was so curious about.

CD
Track 4

Cuquita shook Azucena awake, abruptly interrupting her reverie. Azucena's heart was pounding and she could scarcely catch her breath. When Cuquita saw Azucena's expression, she felt awful about having disturbed her. But she'd had no choice, as they were about to land on Korma. Cuquita could have kicked herself. Azucena's face was deeply flushed, with sweat dripping from her temples. Cuquita was sure Azucena must have been having some erotic dream about Rodrigo. She begged Azucena to forgive her, but Azucena neither saw nor heard her, as she was completely absorbed in her own thoughts.

So, she and Isabel had known each other in their past lives! How could that be? Many years had gone by, yet Isabel looked exactly the same. Things were getting more and more complicated. In that past life, wasn't Isabel supposed to have been Mother Teresa? And how could this "saint" have killed Azucena when she was just a baby? Easy. Because Isabel was no saint. She was a lying bitch who'd deceived everyone, making them believe she'd been Mother Teresa when in fact the Isabel of 1985 was no different from the Isabel of 2200.

Azucena made some quick calculations. If this was the same woman she'd seen during the Mexico City earthquake of 1985 in which her parents had died, then instead of being a hundred fifty years old, Isabel was *two* hundred fifty. Who could have fabricated the life of Mother Teresa for her? Only one person: Dr. Díez! He must have falsified a life for her and recorded it in a microcomputer like the one he'd implanted in Azucena. Things were beginning to fall into place!

Obviously, as soon as Dr. Díez had done what she wanted, Isabel had had him eliminated to keep him from ever telling what he knew. That might in fact be why she had ordered Azucena killed. In addition to being Rodrigo's alibi, Azucena had been witness to Isabel's having lived, as Isabel, in 1985. And something else! She could also testify to Isabel's having murdered her as a baby. No one was allowed to run for Planetary President if he or she had a criminal record, at least in any of the ten lives preceding the candidacy. If anyone ever learned of the murder she had committed in 1985, Isabel would automatically be disqualified.

But something didn't fit. If Isabel had murdered Azucena when she was a baby, then Isabel should know Rodrigo, because in that life Rodrigo had been Azucena's father. And if she knew Rodrigo, why hadn't she just had him killed? Possibly because when she committed the murder, Rodrigo was already dead, and couldn't have seen her. Who knows? And another thing, to what extent was Rodrigo's life in danger now that Isabel had run into him on Korma? One thing was certain: Isabel was extremely dangerous, and Azucena was going to have to keep out of her way.

Azucena took a sip of the warm cornmeal porridge Cuquita was offering her, and immediately felt comforted by it. As an orphan, Azucena had never had anyone who fussed over her. This was the first time anybody had ever done something for her with the sole purpose of making her feel better. She was deeply moved that Cuquita had gone to so much trouble, and from that moment on, she began to love her.

10

Just as a hot glass shatters when filled with an icy liquid, so Azucena's heart burst when she saw Rodrigo. Her soul had not been tempered to receive such a chilling stare. His cold eyes bored into her as if she were a stranger, freezing all her hopes for this reunion.

Finding Rodrigo had not been easy because he kept his distance from the tribe. His constant need to put things in order made him wait to begin his day until the primitives had already performed their slovenly rituals and gone off to hunt. When Azucena found him, he was still inside the cave picking up the discarded sandwich wrappers and folding them one on top of the other. The cave's appearance had changed drastically since his arrival. It was no longer littered with excrement or scraps of food rotting in corners, and the firewood was neatly stacked. At the sight of Azucena, Rodrigo interrupted his work, his attention now fixed on this blonde woman smiling before him with her arms opened wide. He had no idea who she was or where she came from. Clearly she was not from some Kormian cave. It was obvious that, like him, she did not belong there.

Rodrigo's passivity disconcerted Azucena. She could only attribute it to the fact that he had no way of recognizing her in her new body. Pulling herself together, she quickly explained that despite the different body, she was still Azucena.

Rodrigo stared at her vacantly and repeated, "Azucena?"

Now Azucena was truly at a loss. She had dreamed of a romantic meeting in the best movie tradition, where Rodrigo, seeing her from a distance, would run toward her in slow motion: she, in a white chiffon gown undulating in the wind; he, dressed like a twentieth-century heartthrob in elegant linen slacks and a silk shirt half unbuttoned to reveal his strong muscular chest. The background music could only be the theme from "Gone With the Wind." As they met, they would throw themselves into each other's arms, like Romeo and Juliet, Tristan and Isolde, Paolo and Francesca. And then the music of their bodies would become one with the music of the spheres, turning their encounter into an unforgettable moment in the lore of famous lovers.

Instead, there she stood, facing a man who showed not the slightest flicker of life, who had no intention of touching her, who could not stir himself to speak a single word, who refused her the luxury of gazing into his eyes, who was killing her with his indifference and making her feel like a living anachronism. She felt as ridiculous as the sequins on the peasant skirt she'd used on the spaceship to disguise herself as one of the performers at the cockfights: as forced as a beauty contestant's smile, as unwelcome as a cockroach in a wedding cake.

How could this be happening? Had she spent all those sleepless nights waiting for *this?* How could she hold back the kisses longing to escape her lips? To whom could she give her passionate embrace? What could she do with the sweet murmurings stifled in her throat? Azucena turned away from Rodrigo and began running. At the cave's entrance, she bumped into Cuquita, Cuquita's husband, and the body-trafficking *coyote*. She shoved them aside and kept running. Cuquita left the men behind in the cave, and went to look for Azucena. She found her in tears beside a charred tree trunk.

"What's wrong, you feel sick? Me, too. I already threw up. That Julito must think he's a test pilot the way he zooms around in that ship of his. But what's wrong with you? You're crying."

Azucena was weeping bitterly. Cuquita put her big soft arms around Azucena, and hugged her against her pillowy breasts. Azucena sank into them, and for the first time knew how it felt to be cradled in a mother's arms. Unconsciously, she returned to her childhood, and in a childlike voice whimpered all her disappointment to Cuquita, who cuddled and reassured her, as any good mother would.

"So, you scrapped with your fiancé?"

Azucena shook her head.

"Then why are you crying?"

"Oh, Cuquita," Azucena sobbed inconsolably, as Cuquita kept wiping her tears.

"Men are all alike, they should all be pickled by now from the salt of our tears. The philandering bastards! He got himself another sweetheart, right?"

"No, Cuquita, he doesn't even remember me."

"Doesn't remember you?"

"No, he doesn't know who I am. He didn't recognize me."

"Well, why not! You think they laid some *burundanga* spell on him?"

"*Burundanga?!* No, it's nothing like *that!* It's that God doesn't love me. He hates me, He tricks me, He makes me believe in love just so I'd get screwed over like this, but, the truth is, love doesn't exist."

"No, no, don't say that. God's gonna get mad if He hears you."

"Well, let Him. Then maybe He'll leave me alone. I'm sick and tired of Him and His whole choir of Guardian Angels—all they do is crap up my life!"

"Look, haven't you ever thought that what's happening to you maybe *has* to happen?"

"But why, Cuquita? I haven't done anything to anyone."

"Maybe not in this life, but what about the others? You never know!"

"I do so know! And I swear to you, I've already paid off everything I did in the others. This is just plain unfair."

"I can't believe that: in this life, nothing's just plain unfair."

"That's not true!"

"All right, but instead of us fighting over it, why don't you ask your Guardian Angel what he thinks?"

"I don't want to hear anything from him. The reason I am where I am is because he didn't help me, he just let them wreck my life. He abandoned me just when I needed him most. I'm never going to talk to him again. In fact, he'd better not show up, or I'll beat him to a pulp!"

"Hmmm . . . Then we're really in a jam, aren't we?"

"No, we're not! I'm not some helpless idiot!"

"I didn't say you were, and besides, it's completely irreverent to me what you do with your life, but I know there's a reason for everything that happens. Or do you think my grandma's gotta try this in her bones for no reason at all?"

"Gotta try? Gotta . . . *Got arthritis!*"

"Yeah, in her hips! She can hardly walk, and that's from a karma she earned when she was one of Pinochet's generals. But as for you, you need to go way back in your past to find out why all these terrible things are happening to you."

"But I can't. As long as I'm depressed, I can't regress to my past lives."

"Well, then get *un*depressed, because if you don't . . ."

Cuquita's desire to help Azucena was so strong that she became the ideal medium for Anacreonte to convey a message to his protégée. So without any warning, words that were not her own began issuing from Cuquita's lips.

"Because if you don't . . . because . . . what you still haven't realized is that you are living a privileged moment. Caught up in great suffering, true, but it is at moments like these that one can acknowledge that one feels awful. The moment you do, a very real, a very palpable, door is going to open to the possibility of your being able to find inner harmony.

"In this state of openness, you will realize that you can be truly happy on Earth. It is only logical that you don't feel that way now; you have suffered a lot, but soon you will begin to see clearly. You will begin to feel that everything that happens is part of a world in equilibrium. From the rose that comes as a gift, to the stick that is used to beat you. Everything has a reason for being. Why then must people always respond to the stick? The world has become an unending chain of 'He did it to me, so I'll do it to him.' This chain will be broken when one person stops and, instead of responding with hatred, acts with love. That day, you will understand that one can love one's enemy. Countless prophets have told us that. And that day, you are going to laugh at everything that happens to you. You will accept it as part of the whole, and will allow your mind to lead you where it will. Toward the unknown. Toward the beginning.

"Not the beginning of the Earth, which is difficult enough; but toward *the* beginning, which no one yet has reached. For even though man has spoken and written and philosophized so much, he has still not found sufficient strength to go back to the beginning of the beginning. When I met you, I knew you possessed this strength. You are trying to find inner peace and equilibrium by being reunited with your twin soul. You are struggling to find yourself in Rodrigo, which is good. But let me tell you one thing. During that struggle, the person you will truly discover is yourself. That sounds as if it is the same thing, but it isn't.

"It is not the same to recover equilibrium through inner harmony as through union with another person, even if that person is your twin soul. So how will you achieve it? By expanding your consciousness, so that it encompasses everything around you. For example, at this moment you are sad: sadness surrounds you. The external world offers you only pain and suffering. What can you do? Enlarge your consciousness! Appropriate your sadness by drinking it in, sip by sip, inhaling it, capturing it within you, allowing it to spread to the farthest corner of your body until none is left outside. And at that moment, what is going to surround you, once you've let in all that sadness?"

"What?" asked Azucena.

"Happiness, of course! And that is why you must not fear sorrow or pain. You must learn to rejoice in them, to accept them. Whatever you resist, persists. If we resist suffering, it will always be there, surrounding us. If we accept it as part of life, of the whole, and let it enter us until it has run its course, we will be left surrounded with happiness and joy. So go ahead, I wish you well, my child, enjoy it all to the fullest!

"And one thing more before I finish. If you enlarge your consciousness enough to encompass Rodrigo completely, you'll be able to see beyond his rejection and discover why he didn't know who you were."

Cuquita broke off her soliloquy, so impressed she was speechless. She knew all too well that every word she had uttered had been dictated to her. It was the first time she had ever experienced anything like it. Azucena had stopped crying and was staring at Cuquita in astonishment and gratitude. Then she closed her eyes for a moment, and in a quiet, nearly inaudible, voice said, "Because they erased his memory."

"What?"

"Rodrigo didn't know who I was because they erased his memory!"

Azucena was ecstatic. She hugged and kissed Cuquita. Cuquita also celebrated the discovery, but their excitement was short-lived because at the moment Isabel's entourage was heading straight for the cave. Cuquita and Azucena ran to spirit Rodrigo away before anyone realized they were on Korma.

Azucena could not stop staring at Cuquita's drunken husband. It was incredible to think that inside that fat, gross, filthy, alcohol-wasted body was the soul of Rodrigo. The *coyote* had done a superb job. The exchange between Cuquita's husband and Rodrigo could not have been more successful, especially considering he'd had to work under highly unfavorable conditions.

Cuquita was equally amazed as she regarded Ex-Rodrigo from the window of the spaceship. He was wandering among the members of the tribe, completely bewildered. She couldn't believe that she was finally rid of her husband. From this day on, she could sleep in peace. The body exchange had been a terrific idea. For one thing, it allowed Azucena to bring her beloved—or at least, the soul of her beloved—back to Earth with no danger of having the police arrest him for his involvement in Mr. Bush's assassination; and for another, she herself got back her freedom! The sooner the ship left Korma, the happier she'd be.

In the meantime, she watched with glee as a hairy-chested female primitive came up behind Ex-Rodrigo to embrace him. Her husband, thinking it was Cuquita, automatically gave her a whack, to which the female responded by walloping him. Cuquita clapped and cheered, tears rolling down her cheeks. If this was not divine justice, she didn't know what was. For once, someone was giving him a dose of his own medicine. Ex-Rodrigo was laid out on the ground, not knowing what was going on.

He wasn't the only one. On board the spaceship Cuquita's grandmother hadn't a clue as to why they'd seated her beside that "drunken shithead," as she called Cuquita's husband, and no one could convince her that the man she was sitting next to was Rodrigo, not her granddaughter's husband. Being blind, she was guided by smell and sound, and the body beside her, which reeked of alcohol and urine, could only belong to Cuquita's husband Ricardo. They explained the soul exchange to her over and over again, insisting that Rodrigo's soul, which now occupied that body, was very pure. To prove it, they gave him a good sock in the nose. When Rodrigo did not respond in kind, that was all Cuquita's grandmother needed; she began pummeling him for all she was worth to avenge herself for the beating he'd recently given her. She shouted in his face that it was all his fault how sick she was, informing him that to her, he always was and always would be nothing but a "drunken shithead." After venting all her rage, she relaxed into a deep sleep. Finally she could rest in peace.

Rodrigo felt greatly mistreated, emotionally more than physically. Once again he couldn't understand what was going on. The stench coming from his body disgusted him. He was filthy and itched all over. He had a terrible thirst for alcohol and couldn't imagine why, since he himself had never been much of a drinker. He didn't remember ever having seen this old lady who had just beaten him up because he supposedly had mistreated her, and he felt as if he were surrounded by a horde of lunatics on this bizarre spaceship. He did not know where they were taking him, or why.

The only thing he did know was that he had a knot in his throat and a terrible need to urinate. He got up to look for the men's room, but his legs would not support him. The left one buckled completely, as if it were dislocated. Azucena rushed to his aid, telling him to lie down on the floor and asking him if he was hurt. Rodrigo complained of an intense pain in his hip. When Azucena touched him where he was pointing, he flinched. He couldn't stand anyone touching him.

As an experienced astroanalyst, Azucena realized immediately that Rodrigo's pain had its origin in a past life. It came from a hidden fear activated by Cuquita's grandmother's aggression. Azucena spoke to him in a soothing voice, explaining that they were friends who had come to rescue him, and that they wanted to help, not to harm him. They knew about his loss of memory, and they were in a good position to help him recover it, since she was an astroanalyst as well as his . . . his best friend. Rodrigo stared at Azucena for a long time, trying to recognize her, but her face was the face of a stranger.

"I'm sorry, but I don't remember you."

"I know that. Don't worry about it."

"Can you really help me recover my memory?"

"Yes, I can. If you want, we can begin today."

Rodrigo did not want to waste a minute. Without hesitation he nodded yes. The face of the woman who said she was his friend made him feel good. Her voice made him feel safe.

Azucena asked Rodrigo to relax and breathe deeply. Then she directed him to take a series of short, panting breaths. After that she told him to repeat several times in a loud voice, "I'm afraid!" Rodrigo followed all her instructions faithfully. At a certain point, his face and breathing changed. Azucena saw that he was in contact with memories from his past life.

"Where are you?"

"In the dining room of my home . . ."

"What is happening there?"

"I don't want to see . . ."

Rodrigo began sobbing. His face showed great anguish.

"Repeat after me: I don't want to see what's going on here because it's too painful."

"No, I don't want to . . ."

"In that life, are you a man or a woman?"

"A woman . . ."

"And what were they doing to you that makes you so afraid? Who hurt you?"

"My husband's brother . . ."

"What did he do to you?"

"I didn't want . . . I didn't want . . ."

"You didn't want what?"

"For him to . . . rape me."

"Let's go to that moment. What's happening?"

"It was horrible . . . I don't want to see it . . ."

"I know this is painful, but if we don't look at it, we won't get anywhere and you won't be cured. It's good to talk about it, no matter how bad it was."

"I'd just learned I was pregnant and . . ."

Rodrigo's sobbing grew more and more anguished.

"And . . . for me, being pregnant was something so sacred . . . and he destroyed it all."

"How?"

"My husband was drunk, and had fallen asleep. I was clearing the table and . . ."

"Then what?"

"I don't see . . . I can't see anything . . ."

"Say it again: I don't want to see because it's too painful . . ."

"I don't want to see because it's too painful."

"What do you see now?"

"Nothing, everything is black . . ."

Cuquita hadn't been able to hear anything of their conversation, but no detail of their posture escaped her. She was straining so hard to catch a word or two of what they were saying that she began hearing what Anacreonte was trying in vain to transmit to Azucena. Rodrigo couldn't speak for two reasons. First, he had an emotional block not unlike Azucena's, and second, there was an even more serious block caused by a cutoff in the flow of his memory. But if Azucena was able to break through by listening to the music played during her COPE exam, the same might work with Rodrigo, since twin souls react to the same stimuli.

Cuquita waited a minute to see whether Azucena was paying any attention to her spiritual guide, but seeing that she wasn't, decided to offer her services as a professional go-between by passing along the Guardian Angel's message to her: that Rodrigo needed to listen to one of the arias on her compact disc while she recorded his regression with a photomental camera. Azucena didn't know where they could find one, but Cuquita remembered that Julito always traveled with a camera in order to detect potential troublemakers on board. Azucena grew more and more amazed by Cuquita each day. Here was someone she'd looked down upon solving all her problems. The woman was a genius. The two of them lost no time in borrowing Julito's photomental camera, and set it up in front of Rodrigo. In an instant, they had the Discman earphones on Rodrigo's head and began playing him one of the love arias.

CD
Track 5

141

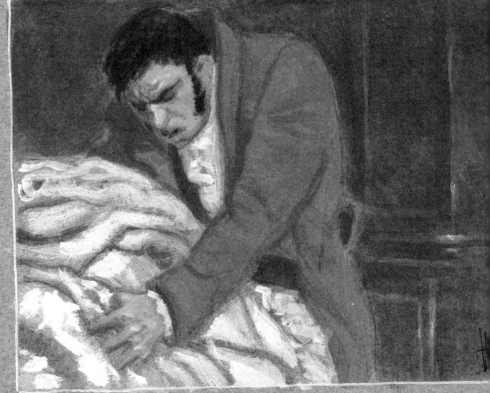

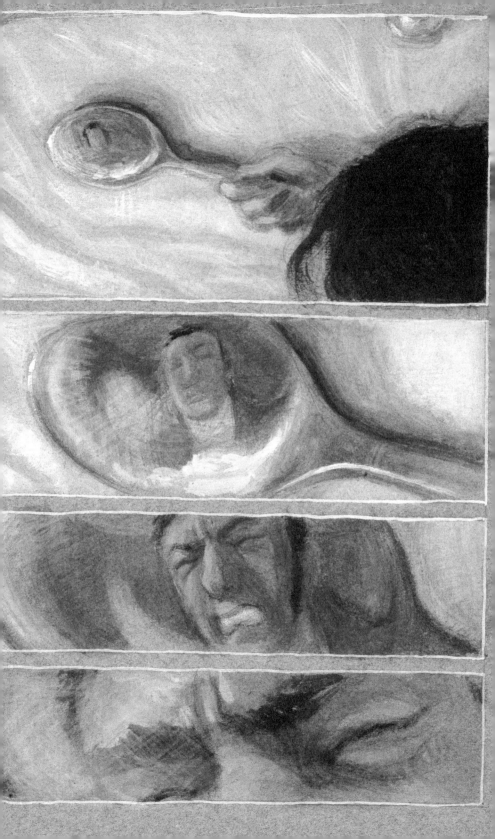

After the last image, horizontal wavy lines filled the camera screen. As a means of escape, Rodrigo had fallen asleep. Apparently, his block was much more powerful than Azucena's had been. Even so, the photomentals she was now holding were going to be extremely helpful. Rather reluctantly, she began leafing through them to see what Rodrigo had recalled. Her first jolt came with the recognition that the dining room he had pictured was the same room that had been her bedroom in her life in 1985. She had recognized the stained glass from the window that had nearly fallen on her the day of the earthquake. With that exception, the difference between the dining room of Rodrigo's life and the bedroom of hers was like night and day. His room belonged to the age of the house's splendor and hers to the time of its decadence.

Suddenly she interrupted her comparisons and held the photomental closer so she could study it in detail. She discovered that the spoon the female Rodrigo had held in her hand throughout the rape was the same one she herself had seen in Tepito, the one purchased by Teo's friend. As soon as they returned to Earth, Azucena would look up Teo and have him take her to his friend. She only hoped the woman still had the spoon. But for now, she had to complete Rodrigo's session and restore him to a state of harmony. She couldn't let him remain in his present condition. Placing her hand on his forehead, Azucena commanded Rodrigo to wake up, so that they could continue the regression. Rodrigo did exactly as he was instructed.

"Let's proceed now to the moment of your death. We're going there so you can understand why you had to have the experience you did. Where are you?"

"I just died."

"Ask your spiritual guide what you needed to learn."

"What it is to be raped . . ."

"Why? Had you raped someone in another life?"

"Yes."

"And how does one feel, being raped?"

"Powerless . . . enraged . . ."

"Call your brother-in-law by name, and tell him how you felt when he raped you."

"Pablo . . ."

"Louder."

"Pablo!"

"He's there now, in front of you, tell him everything . . ."

"Pablo, you made me feel awful . . . you caused me so much pain . . ."

"Tell him how you feel about him."

"I hate you . . ."

"Say it louder. Tell him to his face."

"I hate you, I hate you!"

"How do you feel?"

"Rage, total rage . . . my arms are bursting with rage!"

Rodrigo's face was completely contorted. His veins were bulging, his arms tensed, his fists clenched. His voice was hoarse, unrecognizable, and he wept uncontrollably. Azucena told him he had to scream until he let out all of his buried rage. To facilitate this release she got him a cushion and told him to punch it with all his might. The cushion, however, could not withstand the fury contained in the memory of a rape. After only a few minutes, Rodrigo had pounded it to shreds. The good effect was that his face began to show relief. The bad effect was that everyone aboard the spaceship had moved to one side to avoid being the accidental target of his blows, and the ship, which was not, shall we say, in the very best condition, was destabilized and began to pitch and shudder. Cuquita's grandmother, who had been fast asleep, was awakened by all the commotion. Rodrigo's yelling had pierced her very soul and, still half asleep, she managed to mutter, "I told you, he's still the same drunken shithead!"

Azucena succeeded in calming everyone down, explaining that Rodrigo had discharged all his negative energy and would cause no further problems. They had nothing to fear. All the passengers returned to their seats, and Azucena was able to continue.

"Good, Rodrigo. Very good. Now we must go to the moment when the trouble between you and your brother-in-law began. Because I'm sure that the cause is to be found in still another lifetime. Tell me if you knew him before that."

"Yes . . . a long time ago . . ."

"Where were you living, and what was your relationship to him?"

"He was a woman . . . I was a man. . . . We lived in Mexico City . . ."

"What year was it?"

"Fifteen twenty-one. She was an Indian in my service . . ."

"Now let's go to the moment when the problem surfaced. What's happening?"

"I'm standing atop a pyramid—they call it the Temple of Love—and she comes there, and I . . . I rape her, right there."

"Hmmm . . . That's interesting. Now that you know how it feels to be raped, what do you feel toward her?"

"I feel very guilty at having caused her such pain."

"Tell her that. Summon her. Do you know her in this present life?"

"No, not in this one, but I do in the other one. She was the brother-in-law who raped me."

"I see . . . And now that you know this, do you still hate him?"

"No."

"Then summon your brother-in-law and tell him. Do you know his name in that earlier life?"

"Yes. Citlali . . . Citlali, I ask your forgiveness for having raped you . . . I didn't know how much I was hurting you . . . forgive me, please . . . I'm so sorry for what I did to you . . . I didn't want to harm you . . . I only wanted to love you, but I didn't know how . . ."

"Tell her how you paid for having raped her. . . . Now, move forward in time. . . . Let's go to the life immediately following that one. . . . Where are you?"

"In Spain . . ."

"What year?"

"Around 1600 I think . . . I'm a monk . . . I have a beard and a tonsure . . . I'm trying to subdue my body . . . I'm half naked and waist deep in snow . . . there's a blizzard . . . I'm freezing . . . but I must dominate my body . . ."

Rodrigo was trembling from head to foot; he looked exhausted, anguished, but Azucena had to continue her questioning.

"And are you learning to?"

"Yes. . . . A nun is coming toward me . . . she's taking off her clothes, but I resist . . ."

"What is she like?"

"Pretty. . . . She has a beautiful body . . . but . . . she's a hallucination . . . she doesn't exist . . . my mind has invented her because I haven't eaten in days so that I can conquer my appetites . . . I'm very weak . . . I'm dying . . . I regret having mortified my body . . . wasted my life . . ."

"Why? What did you devote yourself to in that life?"

"Nothing. . . . To controlling my body and my desires . . . but it was so hard, so hard . . ."

"But you must have done something good. . . . Search for a moment that gave you some satisfaction."

"I can't find one . . . nothing. . . . Well, the one useful thing I did was to invent profanities . . ."

"Tell me about it."

"The monks in New Spain did not want the Indians to learn to curse the way the Spaniards did, always saying, 'I shit on God,' and they asked us to invent some new curses."

"Hmmm . . . interesting. Well then, your life wasn't a total waste, was it?"

"Maybe not, but I suffered a great deal."

"Tell Citlali that, back in the life when you raped her. Tell her you had to endure great pain to atone for your guilt. Tell her how hard it was to learn to control your desires. Tell her how you suffered."

Azucena allowed a period of time for Rodrigo to speak mentally with Pablo-Citlali, and then decided it was time to end the session.

"All right. Now repeat after me: I release you from my passion, from my desires. . . . I release myself from your thoughts of vengeance, for I have paid for what I did to you. . . . I release you and I release myself. . . . I pardon you and I pardon myself. . . . I'm letting go of all the rage that bound me to you. . . . I'm letting it circulate freely once again. . . . I release it and allow nature to purify it and utilize it—in regenerating life, in harmonizing the Cosmos, in disseminating love. . . ."

Phrase by phrase, Rodrigo repeated Azucena's words, and as he did so his face reflected his growing relief. He discovered that the pain in his hip had disappeared, and when he opened his eyes, swollen from crying, he had the look of a different person. The atmosphere in the spaceship improved immediately, and everyone was in great spirits for the remainder of the journey.

11

Bells and rattles ring out,
Dust rises as if it were smoke:
The Giver of Life rejoices.
The flowers on the shield unfold their petals,
Glory spreads far and wide,
Binding all the Earth.
There is death here among the flowers,
Here in the middle of the plain!
On the field of battle,
As the war begins,
In the middle of the plain,
Dust rises as if it were smoke,
Turns and curls about
In flowered wreaths of death.
O Chichimec princes!
Heart, be not afraid!
In the middle of the plain
My heart desires
Death by the obsidian blade.
Only this my heart desires:
To die in battle . . .

"Cantares mexicanos," fol. 9 r.
Trece Poetas del Mundo Azteca
Miguel León-Portilla

As fast as the Kormian volcano was spewing lava, Isabel's heart was pumping blood. It was in emergency mode, because the moment Isabel had felt that the lava might overtake her she had begun running like a madwoman, leaving her bodyguards far behind. No one could keep up with her. She ran and ran until finally she passed out. The fear of being burned alive in the seething lava had swept through her body with the force of a hurricane, hurling her soul outward into space. Her body, trying to recover her soul, had raced after it futilely, until it could go no farther and collapsed on the ground.

This was not the first time Isabel had lost consciousness. As a young girl, she had been an accomplished runner, but she had stopped participating in the sport when she realized she no longer had control of her body. Frequently while training, her body, like an untamed horse, would run away with her and not stop until it had used up all her strength. It seemed to happen for no special reason. Of course escaping from the burning lava was reason enough, but generally the impetus wasn't so clear. She seemed to have an inexplicable need to flee, which welled up from the depths of her soul. And now her body, spent by her sudden flight, had fallen not far from Ex-Rodrigo, who himself had lost consciousness at the hands of the primitive woman who had knocked him out with a single blow.

When Isabel's bodyguards Agapito and Ex-Azucena reached her side, they were extremely alarmed by what they saw. Isabel gave every appearance of being dead. What in the world would they tell the Party if that was true?

Ex-Azucena quickly suggested they find someone to blame for Isabel's apparent murder. They thought it expedient to choose a suspect from among the Kormians, who, speaking only that primitive tongue, would be unable to defend himself against the charge.

"How does this one strike you?" asked Agapito, pointing to Ex-Rodrigo.

"Perfect," replied Ex-Azucena, and forthwith initiated Operation Fist.

They were still at it when Isabel came to. The sight of her guards savagely beating the person she believed to be Rodrigo threw her into a fury.

"What the hell are you doing?" she screamed.

"We're interrogating this suspect, boss," was Agapito's quick reply.

"Idiots! Leave him alone!" Isabel struggled to her feet and rushed to Ex-Rodrigo's side where, to her bodyguards' amazement, she began wiping the blood from his nose.

"Are you badly hurt?" she asked.

Ex-Rodrigo, who by then had emerged from the combined fog of his drunkenness and the knockout punch, immediately recognized Isabel as the candidate for Planetary President and clung to her desperately. Tears flowing from his eyes, he implored her: "Señora Isabel, I'm so glad you're here! Help me, please! I don't know what I'm doing here. I live on Earth, my name is Ricardo Rodríguez. My wife brought me here in a spaceship, and . . ."

But Ex-Rodrigo's words were no longer of any interest to her. Leaning back slightly from him to look into his eyes, Isabel realized that this man was not Rodrigo. She shoved him aside and began brushing his filth off her clothing in disgust. Then, to confirm her discovery, she demanded, pointing to Ex-Azucena, "Do you know this woman?"

As soon as he looked at her, Ex-Rodrigo went into a frenzy. "You bet I do! That stinking bitch kicked my balls up my ass. I thought you were dead, bitch! Am I happy to see you again—now you're really going to get it!" Ex-Rodrigo lunged at Ex-Azucena, but he was restrained by Agapito.

"Cool it, sport. You touch this woman and I'll bust what little balls you have left!"

Isabel was deep in thought. She knew that even though she had effectively erased Rodrigo's memory, Azucena's image—the image of his twin soul—must still be embedded somewhere in his mind. However, this man had reacted with total rage, exactly the opposite of what might be expected from a twin soul. That was all Isabel needed to prove to her satisfaction that this "Rodrigo" was indeed someone else. But who? And more important, where was Rodrigo's soul? To find out, she handed Ex-Rodrigo back to her guards, saying, "Proceed with your interrogation!"

It was imperative that Isabel learn who was behind this sinister act that placed her in such danger. She began to tremble. Cold sweat was running down her neck. She could not allow anyone to stand in her way. She *had* to occupy the presidential office, no matter what it took. If not, the era of peace everyone so eagerly awaited would never be achieved. This evidence that she had hidden enemies forced her into the realization that this was war. If she was to win the peace, she had no choice but to do battle.

Unfortunately, her bodyguards didn't have time to extract much information from Ex-Rodrigo because the remaining members of Isabel's entourage were now approaching. It would not be a good idea for them to witness her guards' methods of interrogation. They had only managed to get out of him the names of his wife, her grandmother, Julito, and Chonita, their "new neighbor"—that is, Azucena. Isabel jumped at the mention of a new neighbor.

"This Chonita, did she arrive the same day Azucena died?"

Ex-Rodrigo's reply was a loud affirmative. The fact that the new tenant had arrived the same day they took away Azucena's body couldn't be a mere coincidence, nor could the fact that someone had made away with Rodrigo's soul. Isabel quickly surmised that, before dying, Azucena must have changed bodies. Then she was still alive! And she had somehow come into possession of Rodrigo's soul. Isabel would have to get rid of Azucena at the first opportunity. That was as far as her plans for the future went for the moment. She couldn't determine how to do it just yet, because right now she had to go back to playing her role as saint in front of her entourage.

Everyone was very concerned about her. They had watched her disappear at top speed, running like a soul in torment, but none of them could catch up with her. The attention of one of the female reporters in the group now focused on Ex-Rodrigo. Within seconds, she had recognized him as the alleged accomplice of Mr. Bush's assassin. Isabel immediately intervened to prevent any speculation. She informed everybody present that this was precisely why she had left them so abruptly. She, like the reporter, had a very good eye for faces, and, recognizing this man on sight, she had run after him. He had already confessed to her that he'd been attempting to hide on Korma, but fortunately she had discovered him, and soon he'd be in the hands of the authorities. As a finishing touch, she explained that the bruises visible on his body were the result of a beating inflicted on him by the tribe, who considered him an intruder.

Everyone congratulated Isabel for her bravery, and a series of photographs was taken with her standing beside the "criminal." When Ex-Rodrigo realized that this "dangerous suspect" they kept referring to was himself, he tried to protest and declare his innocence, but with a quick, nearly imperceptible knee to his battered balls, Isabel quieted him. She then ordered her bodyguards to escort the alleged accomplice of Mr. Bush's murderer inside their spacecraft, where he could receive medical attention.

The reporter wanted to beam back to Earth a report on everything that had happened, but Isabel convinced her not to, saying it would hinder the investigation. Any sensational news about the case might alert the other members of this fellow's urban guerrilla gang. The best thing would be to keep it all quiet for the moment, however difficult that might be, and to hand over the suspect to the Planetary Attorney General. His office would conduct a proper investigation and see to the apprehension of the man's accomplices, who were already known to be Cuquita, Cuquita's grandmother, Julito, and Azucena. The reporter willingly accepted Isabel's suggestion, and agreed to delay her story, not realizing she was giving Isabel free rein to act in her own best interests and eliminate the "accomplices" before they were ever arrested.

Who knows whether it was due to the heat, or to their having met with so many obstacles on their return to the ship, but the fact was Ex-Azucena fainted as he boarded the interplanetary spacecraft. Ex-Rodrigo tried to take advantage of his momentary lapse in order to escape, which only brought him another walloping at the hands of Agapito.

Isabel had taken it upon herself to convince everyone that Ex-Rodrigo was an extremely dangerous person and that the wisest course would be to keep him sedated until they returned to Earth. Currying her favor, they had all agreed with her. Knowing that the man could not communicate with anyone had given her a little breathing room. She withdrew, along with her bodyguards, to the conference room of the spacecraft, ostensibly to get some work done.

The truth, however, was that Isabel was playing solitaire, and her much-put-upon guards were reduced to doing nothing but watch. Solitaire was Isabel's passion. She would spend hours and hours shifting the cards around on the computer, especially when she had a lot on her mind. It was as if in arranging the cards she were constructing a dike between the sea and the sand. Or as if in mastering the cards she were mastering her thoughts. Through her game of solitaire, Isabel felt she was transforming confusion into order, chaos into harmony and normality. If only it were as easy to find a suspect as it was to turn over a card. That there was a plan to destroy her, she had no doubt. She had to discover who was behind it before her enemies succeeded in tearing down the image she had labored so hard to construct.

Too bad they weren't traveling directly back to Earth, but she had committed to a stopover on Jupiter. Since the President of that planet was very powerful, it would be greatly to her advantage if they could work out an interplanetary free trade agreement. That would give her enormous credibility and place her far ahead of her opponent in the upcoming election. She couldn't imagine that the negotiations would take more than a day, and as long as Ex-Rodrigo was kept asleep she had nothing to fear. Isabel was confident that no information could be gotten out of the real Rodrigo either, wherever he was. He couldn't possibly recover his memory. At least she hoped not!

What a black day it had been when she fell in love with him. Rodrigo was the one person she had been unable to bring herself to eliminate. And now she was paying the price. She had only herself to blame for being up to her ass in this mess, and it wasn't going to be easy to get out of it clean. She tried to calm herself down, thinking it wouldn't make that much difference if she returned a day late. What *was* certain in her mind, however, was that as soon as she reached Earth she was going to settle accounts with everyone plotting against her. She had already made countless calls from the spacecraft trying to determine who else was in on the plot, but had uncovered nothing. Apparently, Azucena and her co-conspirators were working on their own. Even so, Isabel did not rule out a political plot of wider scope.

Isabel felt fear wrenching her stomach, churning her gastric juices, boring into her intestines. She knew she'd better control herself, but she couldn't. Her thoughts raced on with a will of their own. Unable to restrain them, she continued playing solitaire: to stop thinking; to make order out of something, even if it was only a bunch of lousy cards. Still, they were the only things remaining under her control. Although, now that she thought of it, she did have her bodyguards. She had forbidden the poor creatures to budge or make a sound that might interrupt her concentration, and they were obeying her orders exactly.

This was not the case, however, with Isabel's computer. It had already given her a callus on her finger as she attempted to break her speed record in order to get into the *Guinness Book of World Records*, but the damn thing wouldn't oblige. It just plodded along and couldn't—or wouldn't—follow her rhythm. Isabel was beside herself. She had played several games without winning one. Her heart was pounding, occasionally skipping a beat. If she didn't win she was going to have a heart attack. If only she had a three of hearts! Then she could get rid of the four and work on the next column.

At precisely that moment, Ex-Azucena keeled over with a thud. Isabel leapt from her chair and threw herself down on the floor. She was shaking with fear, convinced that someone had kicked in the door with the intention of assassinating her. Not hearing any shot, she looked up and realized what had happened. Agapito was at Ex-Azucena's side, trying to revive him. Furious, Isabel got to her feet and brushed off her clothing.

"What's got into that moron? Ever since he got that woman's body, he keeps fainting on me."

"I don't know, boss."

"Well, get him out of here. Have the doctor look at him, and then come straight back. Oh, and while you're at it, make sure that our impostor stays sleeping."

Agapito took Ex-Azucena up in his arms and left the conference room.

Isabel sat cursing under her breath. She had been so close to breaking her record, and then that stupid guard had to swoon and screw up everything. Now, even if she played it out, the game would not qualify for the *Guinness Book* because it had been interrupted. It seemed as if lately everything was going wrong, nothing was working out, everything stank. Everything! Even herself. Herself? Yes! That was when she realized that her scare had caused her to fart. It was one of the foulest she'd ever passed. Her colitis was to blame. And the colitis was all Azucena's fault. And Azucena was all . . . whose fault? No matter. The main thing was to get rid of the overpowering stench, or else when Agapito returned he'd find someone else passed out. Opening her purse, she took out an air freshener she carried with her for just such emergencies, and began spraying it around the room. She was still at it when Agapito returned with a troubled look on his face. As he came into the room, his frown deepened; the stench of perfumed fart was nauseating. But being a conscientious bodyguard, he made a superhuman effort and put on a "Me? I don't smell anything" expression. Isabel was relieved, and proceeded to question him.

"What was it? What's the matter with him?"

"Well, he . . . had a microcomputer implanted in his head."

"I thought so! That Azucena is someone to be feared. I wonder what she was up to with that microcomputer? Nothing good, I'll tell you. Well, what's the doctor going to do now, take it out?"

"No, no, he can't."

"Why not?"

"Uh . . . because, well, it might affect . . . uh, because . . . he's pregnant."

"He's what? That lousy hustler? Now he turns into a hooker on me? Get him in here! I have a few things I want to say to him."

"He's right outside, boss."

"Well, what are you waiting for? Bring him in."

Agapito opened the door, and Ex-Azucena entered the room sheepishly. He already knew what awaited him, having heard Isabel's screams all too clearly. When Isabel threw a temper tantrum, no room could contain that voice of an amplified screech owl.

"What's going on, Rosalío? What's all this about your being pregnant?"

"I'm not sure, chief."

"What do you mean, you're not sure? I can't believe you can be so goddamn stupid! Don't you know if you go screwing around like a whore you can end up pregnant? Couldn't you have waited just a few months till I finished my campaign?"

"I swear to you, chief, I haven't had any time for that kind of thing. The only one who I . . ."

Ex-Azucena paused, throwing a frightened glance at Agapito. He was not eager to confess that his cohort was the only person who'd laid a hand on him. Agapito deftly cut in before Ex-Azucena could get the words out.

"Well now, Doña Isabel. Allow me to stick my nose in where it doesn't belong, but I have to say that I don't see how this pregnancy is going to interfere with anything, 'cause it takes nine months for a baby to be born."

"Yes, of course. But how much time is left in the campaign?"

"Just six months."

"And what good is this lousy whore to me for the next half year?

164

Who's going to respect or fear a bodyguard who runs around fainting and vomiting, let alone when his belly starts sticking out!"

Ex-Azucena felt extremely wounded by Isabel's words and tone of voice. After all, this was no way to treat an expectant mother. Unable to hold back any longer, he burst into tears.

"That's just what I needed—for you to start bawling! Get out of here! You're fired, as of right this minute, and I never want to see you anywhere near me again. Understood?"

Ex-Azucena nodded and ran from the conference room.

At the door, he bumped into one of the thought analysts who were part of Isabel's entourage. The analyst regarded the retreating figure with pitying eyes. He didn't even want to imagine what the fate of that guard would be once Isabel saw the photomental shots he'd just taken of him. The whole time Isabel was berating him, Ex-Azucena had been wishing for her to turn into a diseased rat. The photomentals showed, in excruciating detail, Isabel's face on the body of a rat swollen with worms, drinking water from a toilet. Another of the images showed her scurrying through a garbage dump when suddenly a satellite fell on her and she burst into smithereens, releasing a putrid gas. And now as he entered the room, the analyst was astounded, for he believed the bodyguard possessed supernatural powers. It seemed that the fleeing guard could actually produce the same physical phenomena his mind had projected so clearly onto the film. The room really did smell like a dead rat.

CD
Track 6

What kind of thing is love, it seems so much
  like pain,
It never touched me, never touched you,
Never knew how to, or wished to, or tried to.
That's why you aren't with me . . .

Because we never even met
And in all the time we lost
Each one of us lived his part
But each one always apart.
Because you can't extinguish
What has never been ignited,
Because you can't restore to health
Something that never has languished.
Because you'd never understand
My weariness, my manias,
Because to you it'd be just the same
If I fell into the abyss.
This love you've scorned so long
Because you never even looked for me
Where I wouldn't have been anyway,
Nor would you have loved me.

That's why you aren't with me.
That's why I'm not with you.

LILIANA FELIPE

12

How it pains me not to be able to calm Isabel's agitated state of mind. She urgently needs a rest. She's been working like a maniac these last few hours, flashing negative thoughts in all directions; so busy suspecting, plotting, and planning revenge, that for the first time she has rendered herself incapable of following my advice. All that thinking has clouded her mind. Nergal, the chief of Hell's secret police, just paid a visit to bawl me out. He says I have to find a way to tranquilize her as soon as possible. Her rash actions are liable to ruin everything.

I suggested that she take a nice hot bath to relax, but she can't. For some time now, she's been sitting naked on the edge of the tub, too afraid to get into the water. She has never felt secure without her clothes on, anyway. Her love for the movies has merely exacerbated this phobia, because she's seen how as soon as the heroine steps into the shower some calamity befalls her. So that now, when she has real reason to fear an attack, stepping into the tub is the last thing she wants to do. And it would do her so much good! I mean, to relax a little. And that's how I need her, nice and relaxed.

Before any act of destruction there is a period of calm during which the mind becomes clear and decisions can be made. If Isabel does not put a stop to all this activity, that peace will not come to her, and we'll never be able to spring into action. Unthinkable, considering all the things we have to savage and destroy! It doesn't seem possible that Isabel could have forgotten that her mission on Earth is to foster chaos as part of the Universal Order. The Universe cannot allow order to become a permanent condition. To do so would mean its death. Life emerged as a need to balance chaos. Thus if chaos ends, so does life itself.

If all human beings possessed a soul filled with Love, and all were occupying their rightful places, that would be the end of the Universe.

That is why it has been necessary to create such a variety of wars and social conflicts: to distract the human race in its search for order, peace, and harmony. That is why we must fill their hearts with hatred; confuse, torment, exploit them; keep them continually on the run. And that is why we situate them within a pyramidal power structure, so that they cannot think for themselves, so that they always have orders to carry out, a superior above them telling them what to do.

On the day that the cells of Isabel's body are liberated from negative energy, she will be in syntony with positive energy, and will, therefore, be in the proper state to receive Divine Light—which would be disastrous. I will never allow that to happen. And I say that only for Isabel's own good. The human soul is impure. It is in no condition to receive the luminous reflection of God. If that happened in her present state, she would be blinded. And no one wants that, right? Then all of you will agree with me that it is something to be avoided. Generally, the best way of achieving this is to cloud the eyes with that smokescreen the ego, so the individual cannot see beyond himself, nor see any reflection other than that of his own ego projected onto the pupils of his eyes. And if somehow he manages to perceive any glimmer of external light, he will see it as a simple reflector placed there to lend brilliance and glitter to his own person—he will never recognize it as the True Light. That is why it is next to impossible for man to recall where he comes from and what he has to do on Earth. In that state of darkness, it is very simple to align him within an earthly power structure. He will subjugate his will to the service of his superior, and will not offer the least resistance in carrying out his orders.

Orders are transmitted from top to bottom. And who is atop the pyramid? The rulers, of course. And who tells them what to do? We Demons, of course. And who gives us the word? The Prince of Darkness, he who is charged with ensuring that hatred lives on in the Universe. Without hatred, there could be no wish for destruction. And without destruction—I will repeat it a thousand and one times, until all of you learn it—there . . . is . . . no . . . life! Destruction is an essential element in the truly perfect plan for the functioning of the Universe—the very plan Isabel is about to ruin!

I never would have expected it. In numerous lives she has been chosen to occupy the highest position in the power pyramid, and not once has she failed us. She knows how to make people respect her and follow the rule of force. Availing herself of the luxury of cruelty, she imposes her law. She knows how to scheme and intrigue to keep her place on the throne. She knows how to lie, deceive, torture, compromise, deal, and bend the law. Her virtues are beyond number, but the most important may be that she knows how to keep people physically and intellectually occupied, with no time to merge harmoniously with their superior being or to remember their true mission on Earth. And now she's gone and fallen in love! At the worst possible moment, just when we have to engage in the final battle. And God knows what surprise Azucena has in store for us next. I am honestly worried.

When human beings are in love, their minds and thoughts resonate with those of the beloved. And when they settle into that harmonious relationship with love, the door opens to Divine Love, and if this Love filters into their soul, we're lost, since the same will be true for the beloved: once people know Divine Love they want nothing but to experience its presence within them.

Should that happen to Isabel, she would forget she was born to be a destroyer. She would stop working for us and go over to the other camp, to the side of creation, of harmony, of order. The only time we can allow Isabel to put things in order is in her games of solitaire, because when she's occupied with her cards, she slides into a state of mental tranquillity that gives us the perfect opportunity to communicate our instructions. Now, however, not even the solitaire seems to be calming her mind.

After playing for hours and hours, all she has to show for it is a blinding headache. The thought that someone on her team is betraying her is driving her out of her mind. She knows that there must be a traitor somewhere around her; she can't explain how Azucena could still be alive. Someone must have warned Azucena about the plan to kill her, and proposed the solution of a body exchange. So now Isabel has begun to distance herself from all her collaborators, because she sees a traitor in each one of them. She is obsessively studying them in hopes that they will slip up and expose themselves. All this focus on others is preventing her from concentrating on her inner state. She has never liked looking at herself. Not ever. Not even in the mirror. This is logical, because mirrors present the image of what she really is. Usually when people don't like their image, or simply refuse to look at it, they create a reflection of the person they would like to be instead, and by assuming the fictitious image, they no longer see themselves at all.

Wishes act as mirrors. When Isabel says she is determined to destroy Azucena, what she really wants to destroy is herself. That seems fine to me, because I have nothing at all against destruction, but I have to ask myself whether Isabel would agree. Recently it seems that she has forgotten all my teaching and is so filled with fear and remorse that she's afraid to destroy anything. She does not want to accept that it was a mistake to let Rodrigo live—the one weakness she has shown in an entire lifetime. Now she has no choice but to eliminate him, and she doesn't want to.

Her judgment on this and other matters has isolated her from me. Decisions invariably isolate a person from life. Thinking whether I should do this or that, or go from here to there, causes great anxiety. The correct response is always within us, but in order to hear it there must be silence, calm, paralysis. I hope to heaven that Isabel can settle down soon and get over her fear. No one should have any trepidation about what she has done, since the energy of the Universe is always twofold: masculine and feminine, negative and positive. In that energy, Good and Evil are always linked, as are fear and aggression, success and envy, faith and doubt. And that is why no one can ever make the wrong decision. Nothing we ever did can be considered bad if we acted by following our emotions. It will be bad in our eyes only if we allowed judgments to interfere, if our mind makes guilt feel at home. Because if one has set aside reason and connected directly with life, one will discover that there is nothing bad in the Universe, that every particle carries within it an equal capacity for creation and destruction. And more immediately, I, Mammon, exist only because of Isabel's self-destruction. This limits me considerably, for it means that should Isabel lose this capacity, I would automatically disappear from her life. Now *that* would really be a shame!

13

Order was being restored to Azucena's apartment. Cuquita was in the midst of moving back to her own apartment now that there was no obstacle to her living there in peace with her grandmother. Azucena had offered to let them stay with her a few more days, but Cuquita had refused. Azucena kept insisting, but could not persuade her. Azucena's obstinacy was not so much due to a feeling that she'd miss her neighbor as to the fact that Cuquita was planning to take Rodrigo with her.

As for Cuquita, she was making a virtue of her own stubbornness, offering Azucena thousands of reasons why she had to move back and take Rodrigo with her. The most convincing was that as far as everyone in the neighborhood was concerned Rodrigo—or rather the body Rodrigo was occupying—was Cuquita's husband. No one else knew that this big slob of a body housed a good and evolved soul. And it wouldn't be a good idea if people got wind of it, so in order not to arouse suspicion, they'd better have Rodrigo move into the super's apartment with her.

"Honest, you don't have anything to worry about, he's just pure window dressing," Cuquita told Azucena. Naturally, she said it with her fingers crossed behind her back, because beneath that facade Cuquita was nobody's fool and she wanted Rodrigo all to herself. More than anything, she wanted to impress on her neighbors that finally her husband had turned over a new leaf.

Poor Rodrigo. In addition to living in total confusion, he was also the one bearing the brunt of their decisions. The women had told him that he'd have to pretend to be Cuquita's husband, and that although she was not his real wife, she was indeed the wife of the body he was occupying and so it was in his interest to put on the best show possible, since if people learned his true identity his life would be in danger. They had not allowed him to raise any questions, and his amnesia made it impossible for him to pull any weight. The one thing he begged of them was that they explain the situation thoroughly to Cuquita's grandmother, for she still had him confused with Ricardo Rodríguez and consequently would sneak in a passing kick whenever she got the chance.

Rodrigo felt totally out of place. He was not at all pleased with the idea of living with these women who were not his family and who meant nothing to him, and, to top everything off, were making him pay dearly for the favor of hiding him in their house. They were having him pack all their things while they sat back and took it easy. How he longed to have his memory back and to be able to return to his real family; but before that could happen, he needed to work on his subconscious. He desperately needed an astro-analysis session with Azucena! But Azucena kept putting it off, with the excuse that first he had to get all of Cuquita's belongings moved out, so that he could concentrate on the session without feeling any pressure. Well, that was the excuse, but the real reason was that Azucena was waiting for Cuquita and her grandmother to get out of her apartment so she could hold the session alone with Rodrigo, with no busybodies hanging around.

Meanwhile everyone was taking advantage of their last moments together. Cuquita was sprawled out on the bed, enjoying the Televirtual; her grandmother was dozing in the sunlight on the terrace before returning to their cold, damp apartment; and Azucena was using the cybernetic Ouija one last time before its owner left with it. She had put one of the African violet leaves into the flask along with Cuquita's special liquid formula, and she immediately began receiving on the fax images of everything the plant had witnessed during its lifetime. Most of them were totally insignificant, and Azucena was getting glassy-eyed by the time a photo appeared that brought her right out of her chair. It showed the dexterous fingers of Dr. Díez introducing a microcomputer into the ear of . . . none other than ISABEL GONZÁLEZ!

That photograph confirmed several suspicions. First, that that bitch Isabel was no saint! Second, that Dr. Díez had programmed one, if not several, fictitious lives into the microcomputer. Third, that if Isabel had needed a fictitious life, it was because she had a dark past that, were it known, would prevent her from becoming President. And fourth, that the African violet had witnessed the implant. And that wasn't all! It seems it had also witnessed the doctor's murder!

Now the fax was producing highly detailed photographs in which Isabel's bodyguards could be seen altering the cables of the protective alarm system wired to the aerophone booth in Dr. Díez's office, with the express purpose of killing him. Bless Cuquita and her cybernetic Ouija! Thanks to her, Azucena had discovered what seemed to be just the tip of an iceberg. She now had sufficient evidence at hand to incriminate Isabel. She had to put these photos in a safe place.

But first, she wanted to give the African violet a drink. The poor thing was drooping because no one had watered it while she was away on her journey to Korma. She couldn't let it die, the plant was her key witness. Where had it gone? She had last seen it on the table, but it had mysteriously disappeared. Azucena began searching frantically through Cuquita's suitcases. Rodrigo, seeing that Azucena was undoing his morning's work, became enraged, and a terrible row ensued, ending only when Rodrigo finally confessed he had put the plant in the bathtub. Azucena ran to rescue it, leaving Rodrigo muttering to himself.

At that exact moment, the aerophone door opened, and Teo and Citlali walked into the room. Rodrigo was dumbstruck at the sight of Citlali; his face took on the same expression it had the first time he had set eyes on her.

Sometimes, it is a real advantage not to have a memory, because by not remembering the bad things others have done to us, we can look at those people without prejudice. If that were not so, memory would become a powerful barrier to communication. When we see a person who once harmed us, we say: this person is bad because he did such and such to me. We should ignore the past in order to establish healthy ties, and create an opportunity for relationships to develop to the point they are intended. Without memory, prejudices do not exist. Because opinions inevitably draw us toward or away from others, we must know how to set them aside if we are to capture the real essence of a person.

This sounds rather easy, but it isn't. Most people are constantly forming opinions to hide their inability to capture this subtle energy. "She's very high up, you know." "He belongs to the opposition party." "They're not from around here." This creates an insurmountable barrier and we find ourselves dominated by intolerance. As soon as we meet a person, we immediately set out our opinions before him to see how he reacts; if he shares them, we accept him. If not, we try to tear down his opinions in order to impose our own, convinced that the other person is bad because he thinks differently from us. We become narrow-minded inquisitors who in the name of truth put to death anybody whose ideas do not coincide with our own.

We should respect and welcome the opinions of others, even those not in agreement with our own, because ideas are capricious. From one day to the next, our world of beliefs can change, making us aware of all the time we wasted arguing and fighting to the death with someone who—curiously enough—believed what we ourselves now believe. The one constant is Love, unique and eternal. Life would be so easy to bear if only we could look into one another's eyes with the same innocence and vulnerability Citlali and Rodrigo now experienced gazing at each other.

When Azucena returned, African violet in hand, she was paralyzed with jealousy. Tears welled in her eyes as she realized that she, Rodrigo's twin soul, had never inspired such a gaze of perfect love. Teo, gifted with extreme sensitivity, took in the situation at a glance and, trying to ease the tension, hurried to make the formal introductions among Rodrigo, Citlali, and Azucena. Then he quickly explained to Azucena that he had spoken with Citlali as promised and she had agreed to lend her spoon for analysis.

As Citlali handed Azucena the spoon, Cuquita rushed into the room yelling at the top of her voice. Her grandmother snapped awake, cutting short a rumbling snore; Rodrigo and Citlali were shocked back to reality; and Teo and Azucena turned toward Cuquita with expressions of What's going on?

Cuquita motioned for everyone to follow her to the bedroom, where they received the surprise of their lives. There in the room were their televirtualized images. They were being identified as suspects belonging to an urban guerrilla group whose goal was to destabilize universal peace. Strangely enough, the only figure that was not included, the very one responsible for their plight, was Azucena, who possessed an unregistered body that could not be traced.

Abel Zabludowsky was reading a special bulletin:

"Today the Planetary Attorney General released the names of persons belonging to the guerrilla group that has been striking fear into the hearts of the public with its terrorist attacks." The camera zoomed in on Cuquita's husband: "Orders have been issued for the immediate apprehension of Ricardo Rodríguez, alias 'Iguana.'" The camera then focused on Cuquita: "Cuquita Pérez de Rodríguez, alias 'Jalapeña.'" After Cuquita's image came a close-up of her grandmother: "Doña Asunción Pérez, alias 'The Mad Madam.'" And finally the camera showed a still of their old pal Julito: "And Julio Chávez, alias 'Snotnose.'" Zabludowsky continued: "The Planetary Government cannot, and should not, ignore this violation of the Constitution. In order to protect the public and prevent further acts of violence by this guerrilla group, which is a menace to public order, there will be . . ."

Citlali didn't wait to hear more. Grabbing the spoon from Azucena's hand, she apologized, saying she had left beans cooking on the stove, and headed for the door. Teo, defending the accused, tried to convince her to stay a little longer. He did not believe these people were guilty of any offense. This sign of Teo's trust touched Azucena's heart. Every day she had more reason to appreciate this man. Citlali insisted on leaving, promising that she would not tell anyone that she had met them.

"Who did they say the terrorists are?" Cuquita's grandmother asked several times.

"They say it's us, Granny," Cuquita replied.

"You people?"

"Yes, and you, too."

"Me? Go on, you must be kidding! How? When?"

A suitable answer was never given, for at that instant a blast from a bazooka blew out the entry gate to the building. The enemy was literally at their doorstep.

A band of policemen stormed into the building, led by Agapito. With one kick, the door to the super's apartment flew open. Finding it empty, Agapito gave his men orders to comb the building. They rushed toward the stairs. Anyone in their way quickly stepped aside, terrified. Agapito and his men struck out at anybody blocking their path. Suddenly, however, their blows began missing the mark. It took only a few seconds for them to realize that an earthquake was spoiling their aim. Nature is the great leveler, making all humans equal. It has its way with police and civilians alike. Hysterical tenants trying to escape first the officers, and then the earthquake, were scattering down the stairs. Agapito fired a shot in the air. Everyone screamed and fell to the ground. Agapito ordered his men to ignore the tremor and continue up the stairway.

At the first tremor, Julito had bolted from his apartment, not wanting to be crushed inside the building. On the stairs, however, he ran into Agapito and his men. His first thought was that these men had come looking for him. But why? It could have been for any number of reasons. All his life, Julito had been involved in one shady deal after another. His first thought was that it might be best to surrender. The time to settle accounts had finally arrived. Too bad!

He took one step forward, but immediately changed his mind. On second thought, his crimes weren't that serious. Besides, those police were carrying enough weapons to subdue an army, not a poor promoter. He was just being paranoid, they didn't mean him any harm. A rocket from a bazooka passing only centimeters from his head quickly clarified his situation. They hadn't come to arrest him, they'd come to *kill* him!

He had to get out of there, fast. In his desperation, he began running *up* the stairs. On the landing of the third floor he caught up to Azucena, Cuquita, Cuquita's grandmother, Rodrigo, Citlali, and Teo, all of whom, like him, were trying to escape. The first person he overtook was Cuquita's grandmother, who because of her blindness and advanced years was bringing up the rear. Then he passed Cuquita, who was slowed by the cybernetic Ouija she was carrying. Then came Citlali, being forcibly dragged by Teo because she clearly did not want to be caught fleeing in the company of accused criminals. Next was Azucena, who stopped from time to time to wait for the others to catch up. And finally Julito passed Rodrigo, who, since he had no responsibility for anyone but himself, was in the lead.

The stairs were swaying from side to side. The walls seemed to be imitating The Wave undulating around a soccer stadium. At first it seemed as if the tremor was working in favor of the escapees, since it was preventing the police from reaching them, but then it suddenly turned against them. Bricks began to rain down, and steel beams fell across their path. Cuquita cried out for help. Her grandmother couldn't go any farther, and Cuquita couldn't help her because she was carrying the Ouija, which contained their evidence against Isabel. Azucena went back to help. Cuquita's grandmother grasped Azucena's arm and hung on tight. She was terribly unsteady. The stairway, so familiar in memory, was now littered with obstacles. It was terrifying to take a step and find the stair missing, or stumble over a chunk of debris.

Azucena's arm provided firm support. She knew the way well enough to lead the grandmother through the darkness. The old woman, in turn, held on to Azucena and would not let go—not even when her will to live gave out. Azucena did not notice that the grandmother had died, because the aged hand was still gripping her arm with the tenacity of a bureaucrat squeezing a budget.

Neither did she notice when three bullets pierced her own body. The only thing she perceived was that the darkness grew more intense. Everyone vanished from her sight. Her only reality was the tunnel of the dark kaleidoscope she and Cuquita's grandmother were walking through. At the end, she could see a faint glow of light and a few waiting figures.

Azucena began to suspect something strange was happening to her when among those figures she recognized Anacreonte. He received her with open arms. Azucena, dazzled by his light, forgot her old quarrels with him and melted into his embrace. She felt loved, accepted, light as air. The weight of all her problems, her loneliness, and even Cuquita's grandmother, instantly lifted from her.

The grandmother had finally let go of her and was walking toward the light. And not until that moment did Azucena understand that she had died, and she was saddened to know that she had not fulfilled her mission. At last she had remembered what that mission was. When a human being is aligned with Divine Love, knowledge is easily recaptured. What is difficult is to retain that lucidity on Earth, on the field of battle.

To begin with, as soon as one descends to Earth, one loses cosmic memory and can recover it only gradually, in the midst of the daily struggle, with all its problems, necessities, and demands. What happens most frequently is that one loses the way. Just like the general who plans his strategy brilliantly on paper but forgets it all in the heat of battle, when the one thing that interests him is coming out of it intact. Only the initiated know exactly what they have to do on Earth. What a pity that everyone else remembers only when there is nothing they can do about it. What good was it for Azucena to have remembered what her mission was? She had no available body in which to carry it out.

Alarmed, she turned to Anacreonte and begged him to help her.

She couldn't die. Not now! She had to go on living, whatever it took. Anacreonte told her there was nothing he could do. One of the bullets had destroyed part of her brain. Azucena's despair was boundless. Anacreonte told her that the only possible solution was for her to seek authorization to take the body Cuquita's grandmother had just vacated. The drawback, of course, was that the body had a lot of years on it, was not gifted with sight, was racked with aches and pains, and would not be much use in general.

Azucena didn't care. She was truly repentant for having been so foolish, for having broken off communication with Anacreonte, for not having allowed herself to be guided, and for not having cooperated in the important mission of peace to which she had been assigned. She promised to behave properly and to mend her ways if they allowed her to return to Earth. The Gods were moved by her sincere repentance and issued instructions to Anacreonte to give Azucena a speedy review of the Law of Love before they permitted her to be reincarnated.

Anacreonte led Azucena to a glass chamber where he placed in her forehead a brilliant diamond that sparked iridescence as the light struck it. This was a precautionary measure, since Anacreonte was all too aware that tigers do not change their stripes. At this moment, Azucena was feeling very contrite, and willing to do anything, but as soon as she was back on Earth, there was every chance that she would once again forget her obligations and at the least provocation allow the dark veil of obstinacy to settle over her soul, obscuring the way. Now, in case that did happen, the diamond was charged to capture and disseminate Divine Light to the deepest crevice of Azucena's soul, so that there could not be the remotest possibility she would lose her way.

Once the diamond was in place, Anacreonte began—in simple terms and taking the least possible time—to run through the Law of Love, approaching it as a review, not a rebuke.

"My dear Azucena," he began, "every action we take has repercussions in the Cosmos. It would be infinitely arrogant to believe that we are the be-all and end-all, and that we can do whatever occurs to us. We *are* that all and everything that vibrates with the sun, the moon, the wind, water, fire, and earth, with everything visible and invisible. And therefore, in the same way that everything outside us determines what we are, so, too, everything we think and feel has its effect on the external world. When a person accumulates hatred, resentment, envy, and anger within, her surrounding aura becomes black, dense, heavy. As she loses the ability to capture Divine Light, her personal energy goes down, as does—logically—the energy of everything around her. To build up her energy level, and, with it, the level of her life, that negative energy must be released. And how?

"That part is simple. Energy throughout the Universe is one: always the same, yet in constant movement and transformation. The movement of one energy produces displacement of another. For instance, when an idea emerges from the brain, its movement opens a path through the ether and leaves behind it, following the Law of Correspondence, an empty space that must—without exception—be occupied by an energy identical to that creating the vacuum, for it was displaced at that level.

"To give you an illustration, if a thought leaves our brain on the level of a shortwave, we will receive the same energy in return, because the original impulse utilized that level of vibration. This is the same way that a consistent syntony is maintained on a radio station: if what is broadcast, syntonized, is a program of country music, then what you will hear if you are tuned to that frequency is country music. If you want to hear a different station, you have to change the frequency—the syntony. Therefore, if what we send out is negative energy, negative waves of energy is what we will receive.

"All right so far.

"Now, another law says that energy that remains static weakens; and energy that flows grows stronger. Perhaps the best example of this is water in a river and water in a pond. The water of a pond is relatively static, and consequently is restricted in its potential to expand. The water in a river flows and increases to the degree that it is fed by the streams that empty into it along its course. It grows and grows until it reaches the sea. The water in a pond can never become part of the sea; water in a river can. Stagnant water grows foul; flowing water is purified. The same is true of an idea that issues from our mind. As it flows, it increases and will return to us in greater volume. That is why we say that when a person does good, good will be returned to him sevenfold. And the reason is that along the way his goodness will be fed by energy of the same affinity. This is exactly why we should be very careful with negative thoughts, for the same is true of them.

"If people only knew how this law functions, they would not be so driven to accumulate worldly goods. Let me give you a very clumsy example. Let's say a woman has her closet filled with clothes, but she wants to change her wardrobe. First she has to throw out the old clothes or give them away, before she can get new ones, because there's only so much room in the closet. This is precisely what happens in the Universe. The energy moving through it is always the same, but always in constant movement. We are the ones who determine what kind of energy we will allow into our bodies to circulate there. If we store up hatred inside us, like the old clothes, there will be no room for love. If we want love to come into our lives, we must use any means we can to rid ourselves of hatred. The problem lies in the fact that according to the Law of Affinity, as we displace hatred, we receive hatred in return. The only way around this is to transmute the energy of hatred into love before it leaves our body.

"The Pyramid of Love was at one time charged with these functions, and this is why it must be restored. What we are asking of you is a mission that is very nearly impossible, but I know that you can do it. And to make sure, I am going to be at your side at all times. You are not alone. Remember that. You have all of us with you. I wish you well."

With these words, Anacreonte ended what he had thought would be a brief, but turned out to be a lengthy, review of the Law of Love. He gave Azucena an affectionate hug, then accompanied her on the journey back to Earth.

Azucena never really knew how it was that she had managed to escape from Agapito and his accomplices. Her return to Earth in the body of an aged blind woman was truly dramatic—not only because it came at a critical moment, but because it was so complicated to manage this unfamiliar body. The first time she had changed bodies, she had been given a nice new one, and had not encountered any great difficulties. Now, however, the one she had was old and defective. She would have to learn to control it gradually, until she became familiar with its stimuli, its quirks, its pleasures, and its irritations.

She would have to begin by learning to walk without relying on the sense of sight, and to do it on rheumatic old legs. Not at all easy. Not being able to see made her feel absolutely lost. And she had no idea how it was they had escaped Isabel's thugs. The one thing she could be sure of was that a man's hands had pulled her along, helped her to keep climbing the stairs amid the ricocheting bullets and over the countless obstacles in their path. There was a moment when she had collapsed, her body no longer responding to her will. Everything hurt, right down to her soul. Excruciating stabbing pains in her knees had prevented her from getting up again.

The man's hands had lifted her up and carried her to Julito's spaceship, which was docked on the rooftop of the apartment building. She had been blessed with such incredible luck that not a single bullet fired at her hit its mark. Just as they climbed aboard and the door was being shut, a hail of bullets sprayed across the hull. Theirs had been an extremely fortunate getaway. As they reviewed the damage, they found nothing more than a few scrapes and an occasional bruise. With the one exception of Azucena's former body, which was dead, everyone was safe and sound. As the ship lifted rapidly, its passengers let out a cheer.

It was not until the immediate scare was behind them that Azucena began to be aware of what had happened. She was alive! In the body of an aged blind woman, but alive nonetheless. Everyone had welcomed her, and all were happy to know she was still with them. Azucena was deeply moved. Even Cuquita, who had lost her grandmother, was happy for Azucena. She understood perfectly that the old woman had lived her time on Earth, and it seemed only fair that her neighbor should occupy the body her beloved Granny had left behind.

Azucena felt elated. Now all she had to do was learn to get along in the dark. She was so grateful that the Gods had allowed her to return to Earth that she couldn't see the negative side of the state she was in. What's more, she was finding that blindness had its advantages. Forms and colors are very distracting when you want to focus your attention. Her new situation would force her to concentrate on herself, to look inward, to seek images from her past. Besides, out of sight, out of mind: now she wouldn't have to witness the looks of infatuation exchanged between Rodrigo and Citlali. But she had forgotten one small detail. The blind compensate for lack of vision with sharper hearing. To her horror Azucena discovered that, without even trying, she could hear something as delicate as the fluttering wings of a fly—to say nothing of conversations between Rodrigo and Citlali. She could hear all too clearly their flirtation unfolding: the laughter, the come-hithers, the insinuations.

Azucena's optimism ebbed. Like an evil spell, jealousy came back to haunt her once again. Her peace of mind had lasted but a few minutes. Insecurity and doubts returned, taking hold of her mind and plummeting her into depression. She feared she might lose Rodrigo forever. But most depressing of all was discovering that Rodrigo was even more blind than she. Hearing his words, she could tell he was crazy about Citlali. How was that possible? What could Citlali have to offer him? A beautiful body, yes, but no matter how great Citlali's attraction, it could never compare to what she—his twin soul!—could give him. How could Rodrigo waste his time in such petty flirtations? How could he fail to realize that she, Azucena, loved him more than anyone, and could make him the happiest man in the world? From the moment she met him she had done nothing but help him, understand him, lend him her support, try to make him feel good; yet instead of appreciating her, he was letting himself be carried away by Citlali's swaying hips.

Azucena was sure Rodrigo's eyes never strayed from those sensuous buttocks. She had seen him devouring them with his eyes the first moment he met her. That would not have surprised Azucena in any other man. They're all like that, she thought. They can never recognize an ideal woman, they're all blinded by a beautiful ass. She had not expected that, however, from her twin soul, erased memory or not. And what made her angriest of all was that this feeling of being underrated, along with her growing insecurity, was preventing her from dealing with the mess they were all in.

She felt bad for the others. Because of her, Cuquita, Julito, even Citlali, were in up to their necks. Things were getting worse and worse, and she asked herself whether they would ever improve. Even the volcano Popocatépetl exploded in anger. She didn't know for sure, but she suspected that this earthquake had been provoked by the snow-topped volcano. Popocatépetl had done that on previous occasions. It was his way of showing his disgust over the current political situation, a warning that events were not going well.

The one thing that calmed Azucena was to think that his spouse, the volcano Iztaccíhuatl, had not been infected by her mate's anger, for she was the one who was truly in charge of the destiny of the nation, and of every Mexican in it. Popocatépetl had always acted as her prince consort. It was she who reigned. Her enormous responsibilities kept her very busy and distracted her from the small pleasures couples normally share. She could not allow herself the luxury of yielding to the gratifications of the flesh, because she had to watch over all her children.

One of the legends of the Indian past recounts the relationship between the two volcanos. Iztaccíhuatl's husband Popocatépetl looks upon her as a great lady, and respects her enormously, but as he needs to vent his passion from time to time, he has taken a lover, Malintzín. She is very seductive and sweet, and he passes many happy moments in her company. Iztaccíhuatl of course knows about their love trysts, but does not take much notice of them. She has more important matters to attend to. The fate of a nation is a serious burden. She has no interest in punishing Malintzín. Actually, she is grateful to Malintzín for keeping her husband happy, since she herself can't. Well, it isn't that she can't. Obviously she can, and would do a better job than anyone else! She simply isn't interested. She prefers to maintain her grandeur, her power, and her dominion, letting Malintzín tend to lesser matters, those appropriate to her station. In Iztaccíhuatl's eyes, Malintzín's talent is limited to the bedroom. She makes sure that Malintzín remains in that category, and otherwise ignores her completely.

It seemed to Azucena that if Rodrigo was to have his Popocatépetl syndrome, and entertain himself with his Malintzín, it was only fair that she should enjoy the Iztaccíhuatl syndrome. After all, at this moment she was responsible for several people's fates. She had major problems to resolve, but all she could think of was losing Rodrigo's love. With all her heart and soul, she appealed to the great Lady Iztaccíhuatl for help. How she wished for a little of that lady's loftiness. It would be such a relief not to feel that passion tormenting her, burning her up inside. How she wished to be free of the anguish of hearing the flirtatious tone in Rodrigo's voice, and to find the inner peace she so desperately needed. How she longed to feel a man's arms around her. To feel a little love!

Teo walked over to Azucena and very tenderly embraced her. He seemed to have divined her thought, but that was not quite the case. In fact, Teo was acting under Anacreonte's orders. He was one of the undercover Guardian Angels Anacreonte had assigned to Earth. He called on them in cases of extreme necessity, and this was certainly one of those! They could not allow Azucena to become depressed again.

Azucena did not resist Teo's embrace. At first it communicated protection and shelter. She leaned her head against Teo's shoulder. With great tenderness, he stroked her hair, and kissed her softly on the forehead and cheeks. Azucena lifted her face to make it easier for him to kiss her. Her soul began to feel soothed.

Timidly, Azucena returned Teo's embrace with another, his kisses with her own. The caresses between the two gradually increased in intensity. Azucena was madly sucking in the male energy Teo was supplying her and that she had such need for. Teo took Azucena by the hand and gently led her to the ship's bathroom. There they closed the door and gave free rein to the mingling of their energies.

Teo, being the undercover Guardian Angel he was, had achieved a very high degree of evolution. His eyes were conditioned to see and to take pleasure from the surrender of a soul like Azucena's, even one inside a body as decrepit as that of Cuquita's grandmother. Slowly, Azucena took possession of that aged body, and pushed it to work harder than it had in many, many years. To start with, Azucena's jaws had to open much farther than usual to receive Teo's tongue in her mouth. Her dry, wrinkled lips had to stretch, though they were aided in this by saliva from her astral companion. Her leg muscles had neither the strength nor the flexibility required for the act of love, but nearly miraculously, they acquired them in short order. At first she had leg cramps, but once they warmed up, they worked quite well, like those of somebody much younger. The inner core of her body, moistened by desire, permitted penetration to occur not only comfortably but indeed pleasurably. Her body remembered once again the agreeable sensation of being caressed inside, over and over.

The enjoyment Azucena was experiencing so opened her senses that she was able to perceive Divine Light. The diamond Anacreonte had placed in Azucena's forehead was working perfectly as planned, magnifying the light that blazed at the moment of orgasm. Azucena's barren soul was left radiant, refreshed, budding with love. Its desert-like thirst had been finally assuaged. It was not until she was loved that she knew peace . . . And it was not until she heard the desperate banging on the door—Cuquita needed to use the bathroom—that Azucena returned to reality.

When the door opened, and Teo and Azucena walked out

together, all eyes were turned to them. Azucena couldn't conceal her happiness. It was visible a mile away. Her cheeks were rosy and her expression full of contentment. She actually looked lovely, imagine! But naturally, despite how well her body had performed during the heat of passion, nothing was going to help her the next day. Every inch of her body would ache—even her eyelashes. No matter, making love had fulfilled its purpose. For a moment, Azucena had been aligned with Divine Love. That was enough to give her the urge to work on her subconscious once more.

Whistling a tune, she strolled down the aisle of the spaceship on Teo's arm. As soon as she reached her seat, she sank down with a deep sigh, got out her Discman, and awaited her regression in a state of total bliss.

CD
Track 7

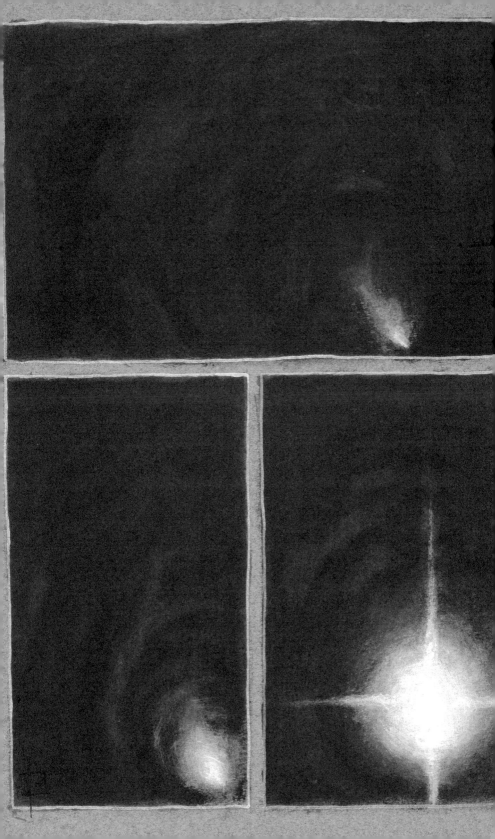

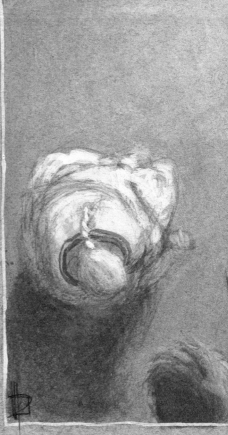

Azucena opened her eyes too soon. She was breathing fast, and had emerged from the regression in a disturbed state of mind. She realized that the woman who screamed so desperately over the death of her child was none other than Citlali, and that the baby boy who lived but a few minutes was none other than herself in another life. She was deeply moved to learn that this woman she was so jealous of in her present life had been her mother then. She could no longer look at her in the same way. Or at Rodrigo. It was truly a shock to learn that Rodrigo, her adored Rodrigo, the man she was prepared to do anything for, was the Conquistador who had killed her in cold blood.

It had taken a moment for her mind to connect the image of Citlali with that of the Indian woman Rodrigo had raped. They were one and the same! She was certain, because she had examined the photomental of the rape countless times. She knew that face by heart. The photomental had been part of Rodrigo's regression, and Azucena had morbidly held on to it. How many times had she succumbed to the torment of seeing Rodrigo possessing another woman, seeing the lust in his eyes. Now she would consider that image from a different perspective. It must have been traumatic for Citlali to have been raped by the same man who murdered her son. What a horrendous experience! Azucena felt a deep sympathy for her.

Teo immediately understood what Azucena was feeling. Putting his arm around her, he quietly consoled her, and his gentle words had their effect. Azucena relaxed and slipped back into the Alpha state. He suggested that Azucena ask what her mission had been in that life. Meekly Azucena followed his instructions. After a pause she replied that it had been to inform the Aztecs of the importance of the Law of Love, because in breaking it, they were courting danger and could suffer the consequences of the Law of Correspondence. Teo asked Azucena if she had been able to deliver that message. She shook her head, explaining that she'd been murdered before she could pass it on. She spoke of having had another occasion to deliver that message, in 1985, but again she was prevented from doing so. Now Azucena understood that she was being given another opportunity to say what must be said.

At that moment Azucena began to comprehend the reason for everything that had happened. She discovered that there is a logic to all events; everything that happens is the result of some prior occurrence. Following that logic, there is no such thing as injustice. For her, the only question that remained was, why me? Why hadn't they chosen someone else to deliver such an all-important message? She could find no answer, but at least she was now aware of her mission, and had regained her enthusiasm for carrying it out.

But now, too, she had the bad luck of having a new impediment: she could not return to Earth because she, along with everyone else on board the spaceship, was being sought by the police. She was mulling over that problem when Cuquita brought some important news. She had just heard on the radio aboard that a group from several planets was making a pilgrimage to La Villa, in Mexico City, to worship at the shrine of the Virgin of Guadalupe. If they could somehow infiltrate that crowd, it would be impossible for anyone to detect their return to Earth. Azucena was thrilled by this news. She consulted with her companions, and they all agreed to abandon the *Interplanetary Cockfight* on the nearest planet, and travel on the huge spacebus carrying the pilgrims.

CD
Track 8

San Miguel Archangel, little saint,
Don't be so hard, so silent,
Don't go on rejoicing in your past
When it's now I really need you.

Now's when the devil's heating up,
Now's when the saints, there ain't so many,
Now's when the gods are all good-byes,
And sin strolls around so easy.

San Miguel Archangel, little saint, little saint,
San Miguel Archangel, little saint,
Don't stand there like you're made of stone,
While I'm dragged down by disillusion.
I cry cry cry, can't sing anymore.

Now's when Mephisto's ringing my bell.
Now's when the fat cows are growing skinny.
Now's when bribes are a dime a dozen.
And life's pushing me over the edge.

San Miguel, little saint, little saint . . .

LILIANA FELIPE

14

Really, there's nothing I can do about Azucena. No matter how much help you give that woman she always goes and craps things up!

I swore to abide by the Law of Love, and to see that others did the same, and here I am on the verge of breaking it. I'm no longer capable of administering justice. I'm running short on ethics and, what's worse, I feel like the ultimate cynic, sitting on a Guardian Angel throne when in my heart all I want is to be done with the whole lot of those bastards—beginning with Isabel and ending with Nergal, the chief of Hell's secret police!

I thought that with the help of Teo, Azucena would pull herself together and carry out her mission. But no! All she's done is go and fall head over heels in love with him like some teenager, and she can do nothing now but think about him. No, there's no doubt that everyone is playing their part very well—except me! Teo, our undercover Guardian Angel, is *too* efficient, the rascal! He's having the time of his life backing Azucena into corners and pawing at her. His excuse is that he's doing it to keep her pointed toward Divine Love, but the pointer he's using is something else again.

And I'm stuck here like an idiot, while Nergal removes Mammon from his post as Isabel's Devil; and Mammon, who now has all the free time in the world, starts flirting with my sweetheart Lilith. Meanwhile, Azucena, full of romantic ardor, is plotting an armed revolution with Julito that will put an end to Isabel once and for all. God help us!

Since Azucena refuses to look inside herself for answers, she is centering all her attention on finding solutions to other people's problems. Why not! It's a lot easier to see the speck in someone else's eye. Fear of having to plunge right into her own gut, a real terror of mucking around in the shit, has pushed her to look for a collective solution to her problem—forgetting that collective solutions don't always work, because every person must attend to his or her own spiritual evolution. No social organization will ever be able to find the one road that's good for everybody, because Azucena's everyday problems—like those of the rest of humanity—are the result of errors that were left unresolved in the past. Each case is unique. Of course, such errors affect the person's participation in the outside world, but it's not by changing the social order that one's problems are resolved. It's by changing ourselves. When that happens, society is automatically modified. Every internal change has repercussions in the external world.

So what must be changed internally? The answer is found in the past. If we are to overcome them in this lifetime, each person must discover which problems could not be solved in other lives. If not, these problems will remain bound to the past with ties that sooner or later will be converted into chains that will prevent us from carrying out the mission in our present lives. Knowledge of the past is the only way to free ourselves from those chains and to fulfill our mission—our unique, our untransferable, our personal mission. Who the devil told Azucena that organizing a guerrilla war is going to solve all her problems? Wars or revolutions, even though they are sometimes needed and sometimes attain their objective of benefiting society, can also adversely affect individual evolution. Such is the case with Azucena at this particular moment: any activity of that sort will only distract her from her mission.

There are other obstacles to the fulfillment of Divine Will. The most common, and the most damaging, is the Ego. Everyone in the world likes to feel important and appreciated, recognized and honored. To achieve that, they usually make use of the gifts nature has given them. The praise they receive from their writing, their singing, their dancing, their national leadership, makes them forget the reason they were granted those gifts. If they were born with special talents, it was not for personal glory, but because with those gifts they were to serve Divine Will.

Azucena's gift for organization is the primary weapon she can count on if she is to succeed in her mission, but, paradoxically, the way she's going, it'll turn out to be her worst enemy. She's so full of herself right now—caught up in Julito's praise of her skills and intelligence—that she is directing all her free will toward making decisions that will lead to a victory over Isabel. A victory that obviously will mean additional praise for Azucena, but one that will divert her more and more from her mission.

Why is that? Because if she triumphs, she will then be a government politician. Power will convince her that she is a very important woman. Feeling important, she will believe that she is deserving of all kinds of honors and recognition. If she doesn't obtain them immediately, she will feel offended, hurt, and diminished, and will hate the person or persons who've denied her recognition. Why? Because to this day, no one in power has ever reacted differently. That's why. And afterward? She will try to hold on to power any way she can. By scheming, murdering, and—in a word—hating! Resentment will coat her aura with a thick layer of negativity.

The more resentment that accumulates, the less able she will be to hear my counsel, because such messages travel on very subtle vibrations of energy that will be blocked by the curtain of praise that keeps her trapped in self-delusion. Then what? Then we will never exchange another word. That curtain will seal off relations of any kind, and I'll be out in the cold. Me, her Guardian Angel! The one she should in fact be seeking recognition from, not that jackass Julito! What a jerk!

But what am I saying! Here I am insulting an innocent man. It's just that Azucena is beginning to push me over the edge. If she doesn't come around soon, I'm afraid I'm going to end up losing my mind. What I most resent is that because of her I'm losing Lilith. That I can't take! Oh, I know that this, too, is a vulgar problem of ego, and that it's best to set it aside so that it doesn't prevent me from accomplishing my mission with Azucena, but what can I say? I can't control myself. How embarrassing! I know what a pitiful spectacle I must make. A Guardian Angel sick with jealousy—what a perfect story for the tabloids! What makes it even more incredible is that I wrote my doctoral thesis on how a deformed ego can ruin a relationship. Believe me, I know it all by heart.

A person with an ego problem will want as a partner someone who is a prized and valuable object. The most handsome or beautiful, the most intelligent, and so on. An object that only he possesses, because if everybody had the object, it would lose its value. Once he has acquired it, he will take meticulous care of his property to make sure that no one else touches it, that no one steals it, because if it is lost, his ego will feel diminished. The partner is thereby converted into a mere article that confers status and evokes admiration. The egoist will never for a minute wonder whether the object-partner was the one indicated in the Divine Plan. The perfect partner could have walked right by the egoist without even provoking a second look, because he did not possess an observable talent, or muscles, or she was not sufficiently beautiful, or intelligent. This inability to probe the depths of the human soul prevents the egoist from recognizing that partner; instead, the voice of the ego urges him to choose someone not meant for him.

The only way to resolve such mistakes is to convert a negative ego to a positive one through self-awareness. When we know ourselves truly well, we learn to love ourselves and to value ourselves for who we are, not for who our partner is. This love will change the polarity of an aura from negative to positive, and then, thanks to the Law of Correspondence, we can attract the person we were meant to be with in our lifetime. We'll no longer feel unhappy if someone rejects us, because we'll understand that attractions and rejections have to do with karmic law, and not with our value as human beings. Our ego suffers if somebody rejects us, but if we overcome that rejection through knowledge, we will realize that we ourselves are responsible for having broken the Law of Love, and that the only way to restore balance is through Love.

You see? I know it by heart. But that doesn't stop me from being all screwed up.

Shit! Here comes *my* Guardian Angel. That's all I need. He always shows up when our line of communication is fouled, and when I'm behaving like an idiot. But what is it I'm doing wrong? The one who's pissing outside the pot is Azucena, not me. Or *is* it? Maybe I have it backwards and I'm being as big a fool as she is. Maybe I've been waiting for her to change and make everything all right, when the one who needs to change is me. What a fool I am!

So now what do I do?

15

The prayers of the thousands of people traveling in the enormous spacebus filled Azucena's heart with hope. So much faith concentrated in such a relatively small space was contagious. The heat of the votive candles and the smell of incense generated a feeling of warmth, innocence, purity. Azucena felt younger than ever. Her cheeks had taken on a rosy color; her aches and pains had disappeared, and she had completely forgotten her blindness, her arthritic hands, her sciatica. Her relationship with Teo made her feel secure, loved, and desired. She knew it did not matter to him that her skin was wrinkled, that her hair was gray and her teeth not her own. He loved her just the same.

No one can deny that this business of being in love does wonders for a person. Life changes completely. Azucena, cuddled in Teo's arms, felt like the youngest, most beautiful woman in the world. She asked herself whether her emotions were unique, or whether this often happened with people of advanced age. What did it matter if the body was old? The person was the same inside. The desires were the same.

But at the thought of her desires, Azucena suddenly remembered Rodrigo. She had completely forgotten him! That was logical, because with all the kissing she'd been doing, it wasn't easy to remember anything. Besides, Teo had taken it upon himself to convince her that Rodrigo truly loved her more than anyone in the world, and that the only problem was he didn't remember that. Like any other woman, once she accepted that her lover loved no one but her, Azucena was able to tolerate his infidelity. She understood that if Rodrigo felt attracted by Citlali it was because of a fleeting passion in a different life, and that as soon as his reason returned, he would come back to her forever.

Meanwhile, she was getting along famously with Teo, and had no guilt about doing so. Teo had a very interesting theory about fidelity, which she had come to share. He said that a partner is good for someone as long as one's heart is inflamed with love. However, the day the relationship produces hatred, resentment, or any kind of negative emotion, rather than being advantageous, it holds back individual evolution. The soul fills with darkness, and that person can no longer see the path that ultimately will lead to the twin soul, and the recovery of Paradise.

It certainly suited Azucena for Citlali and Rodrigo to be in love, because Rodrigo's infidelity would bring him back to her sooner. In the end, a person spends fourteen thousand lives in which he is unfaithful to his original mate, but, paradoxically, infidelity is the one way to return to her. Of course, this is not infidelity for the sake of infidelity. The love that makes us evolve is the product of a total surrender between two parties. This is the love that grows within a closed circle containing male and female, *yin* and *yang*, the two indispensable elements for the generation of life, pleasure, and equilibrium. When we are in love, we should devote ourselves only to that person, and the more in love we are, and giving of ourselves, the more energy will circulate and the more quickly we will evolve.

But if, say, the man decides to break his circle of energy to make a connection with a new lover, a large part of the energy he had generated will, unavoidably, escape. In those instances, infidelity is damaging. Nevertheless, that does not mean that one must remain faithful to one partner for a lifetime. No, the union should last only as long as loving energy flows between the two partners: once it is no longer present, we should search for a different partner. In sum, the solution is infidelity, but a qualified infidelity. The objective is to keep oneself filled with the energy of love, just as Teo and Azucena were.

Teo, after having spent the night consoling Azucena, was near exhaustion and had fallen asleep. Azucena, on the other hand, was brimming with energy. She jumped out of bed and went to look for Julito, so that they could continue their work on the plan to remove Isabel from power. Azucena was worried that she would never be able to return the capstone of the Pyramid of Love to its rightful place as long as Isabel stood in the way. Why? Simply because Isabel was a total bitch, and only by getting her out of the way would Azucena be free to act.

She found Julito in a remote corner of the ship, working on a bottle of tequila. Azucena sat down beside him. His choice of location was perfect: as far as possible from all the others—the farther the better. That way they could work on their plan without being overheard. Well, that wasn't the only reason. The truth was that Azucena never felt comfortable in crowds. She preferred intimate spaces. Exactly the opposite of Cuquita, who was like a fish in water when surrounded with people. The more there were, the better she liked it.

Azucena was convinced that the great majority of Non-Evos shared this trait. It didn't matter how different they might be in physical appearance, they behaved in a similar way throughout the Cosmos. They understood each other. Azucena was always amazed at the quick ease with which Cuquita related to everyone. In the short space of time they had been traveling with the shipload of pilgrims, she already knew nearly all their life stories. It was incredible how she had been able to put her grandmother's death behind her. Azucena believed that part of it might be that Cuquita could still see her grandmother. She hadn't had time to feel she'd lost her, because in fact she hadn't. Her grandmother wasn't exactly there, but in a way she was; bearing Azucena's soul, but still alive.

Whatever the reason, it was fortunate that after everything that had happened, Cuquita hadn't lost her sense of humor. She wandered around from group to group, poking into all the conversations. One of the groups was arguing over whether someone had taken a shot before or after . . . the other was struck in the head? Cuquita thought they were talking about the Bush assassination and ran over to hear the latest bit of gossip, but she was disappointed to discover they were arguing about the finals of the Interplanetary Soccer Championship between Earth and Jupiter—in which Earth had lost. Cuquita was of the opinion that the person responsible for the loss was the trainer, because he hadn't played Hugo Sánchez. They should have paid attention to his wife, who kept screaming from the stands, "Put him in, put him in!"

That was the tenor of the conversation when someone asked Cuquita whether she knew anything about Mr. Bush's murder. That made her a little nervous, but as she didn't want to arouse their suspicion, she took a deep breath and prepared to give a suitable answer. As was her way, her comments began normally enough. In a loud voice, she warned everyone present not to let themselves be swayed by the news programs, because the people who had been accused of the crime were nothing more than the sacrificial limbs of the system. Everyone was satisfied with that explanation and apparently no one noticed that Cuquita got her words mixed up, or, if they did, they didn't seem to mind. Well, Azucena thought, "Birds of a feather . . ."

Once the pilgrims saw how well informed Cuquita was, they asked her opinion about the direction things were taking in Mexico. What worried them most was all the recent violence. Cuquita agreed, saying she hoped that soon they would discover whose Macrobellian mind had planned those horrible murders.

"Murders? We thought there had only been one—Mr. Bush's. Were there others?"

Azucena was getting upset. She was going to have to find a way to silence Cuquita, or else she'd spill everything and sink them all. So Azucena asked Julito to lead her over to Cuquita in order to defuse the conversation, but by the time she reached her side, it was no longer necessary: Cuquita had smoothly switched to a different topic and was entertaining her audience with a theory about why Popocatépetl had vomited. She told them that in case they didn't know, the volcano absorbed the energy and thoughts of everyone who lived on Earth, and that recently he had been feeding on a diet of shock and violence, which was why he'd developed indigestion and belched up the sulfurous blasts that accompanied the earthquake they already knew about. The pilgrims were astounded by Cuquita's explanation, which made them even more convinced that things in Mexico were growing worse. If Popocatépetl was that steamed up he might set loose a chain reaction among all the volcanoes connected to him through underground channels, thereby provoking a world catastrophe that would affect not only the inhabitants of Earth but everyone in the Solar System.

If only Rodrigo hadn't gone off with Citlali, Azucena might have been less sensitive to the pain of the gravel digging into her knees. She and her companions had been on their knees a long time, still masquerading as pilgrims, inching forward with the thousands trying to enter the Basilica of the Virgin of Guadalupe. So as not to awaken suspicion, they had decided to wait until after the Mass to break away from the worshipers. The only ones who had risked leaving were Rodrigo and Citlali: Citlali because she urgently needed to get back to her house; and Rodrigo, to follow her. In addition, Citlali could not see any reason why she should remain with this dangerous group, since neither Rodrigo, in the body of Cuquita's former husband, nor she, was being sought by the police.

Before they left, Azucena, feigning indifference, had quickly bid them farewell. Teo knew very well, however, that she was torn up inside. Supportive as always, he had not left her side, lending his great physical and spiritual support. Had it not been for Teo, who knows how Azucena could have borne the loss of Rodrigo. She was able to tolerate his infidelity as long as he was near her, but not when he was gone.

With great tenderness, Teo attempted to make up for Rodrigo's absence, guiding Azucena along the easiest route to El Pocito. This was a natural spring where from time immemorial the Aztecs had purified themselves before offering tribute to the goddess Tonantzin. The ritual had continued, uninterrupted, from the time of the Conquest, but for some time it had been performed in honor of the Virgin of Guadalupe. The purpose of this ceremony was to remove all impurities of thought, word, and deed before entering the Basilica, by washing one's face, hands, and feet in the pool. Teo, the perfect guide, avoided obstacles of every kind as he led Azucena to the edge of El Pocito. She leaned over and cupped water in her hands, but before she could splash it on her face to purify herself, Cuquita hurried up to her and whispered:

"Don't turn around, but right behind us is that guy who's been using your ex-body."

Azucena's heart jumped. That could only mean that Isabel's men had already caught up with them.

A split second later, Cuquita, Azucena, and Teo were on their feet and moving through the crowds, with Ex-Azucena hot on their heels. It was nearly impossible to push through the oncoming throngs, especially for the blind Azucena. Teo decided to pick her up and carry her, since she had already stepped on at least six people moving toward the shrine on their knees. After only a few minutes of pushing through the masses of people pressing toward them, they had lost Ex-Azucena, but then bumped into two policemen who regarded them suspiciously and began following them. Teo, still carrying Azucena, who had fainted, picked up speed and told Cuquita to follow as he zigzagged through the crowds. He knew his way around this part of the city because he had grown up here. When they came to a certain corner, he beckoned Cuquita into an abandoned building. Laying Azucena down on the floor, he softly began to kiss her forehead. Azucena regained consciousness. Teo put his hand over her mouth to keep her from making a sound that might betray their whereabouts to the two policemen, who had stopped in front of the door to the building. Cuquita, contrary to her nature, also kept quiet. The only thing they could hear was the pounding of their hearts, the loudspeaker of a spacecraft announcing the Televirtual debate between the European and American candidates for Planetary President . . . and Ex-Azucena's sobs.

Teo and Cuquita whirled around and spotted him hiding there in the shadows of the ruined building. He looked bedraggled and terrified. As soon as he saw that he had been discovered, he motioned for them to remain quiet. Teo whispered to Azucena what was happening. She was shocked to learn that the bodyguard seemed to be in the same predicament they were.

As soon as the police moved on, Cuquita gave Ex-Azucena a piece of her mind.

"So now it's the big crybaby, eh? Well, what about when you were going around liquefying everybody? So you thought the police were never going to find you! Hey, wait a minute. If the police know you're the one who had a body change after you killed Bush, then they also know that we're innocent. So, now *you'll* see, I'm turning you in!"

Cuquita began heading for the doorway to call the police, but Ex-Azucena pulled her back.

"Hang on a minute! The cops still believe you're the ones who killed Mr. Bush, and if they see you here, they're going to drag you off to the slammer, I can tell you . . . Honest, it won't help you to turn me in—it's not the police I'm hiding from."

"Well, who *are* you hiding from?" asked Azucena.

"Isabel González."

"But isn't she your boss?" Cuquita wanted to know.

"She was, but she fired me. Oh, it was just horrible—and all because I'm pregnant."

Azucena was livid. This ex-ballerina bodyguard, thanks to having *her* body, was now going to have a baby. The lousy bitch! Envy flooded Azucena's soul. How she longed to have her own body back, to experience pregnancy, which was forbidden to her as long as she was in the body of Cuquita's grandmother. Anger shot straight to her head, like wine, and before Teo could stop her, Azucena leapt upon Ex-Azucena and began scratching and clawing.

"You slut! How dare you get pregnant in a body that doesn't belong to you!"

Ex-Azucena bent over to protect his belly. It was all he could do. There was no hope that he could fight back against the pummeling he was taking from the crazed old woman.

"I didn't get it pregnant, it was already that way!"

Azucena stopped dead. "Already that way?"

"Yes."

Blood pounded in Azucena's temples, and for a moment she was as deaf as she was blind. If that body was already pregnant before the bodyguard took it over, then the baby this man was expecting was hers—she had conceived the child with Rodrigo during that one marvelous night of their honeymoon. Azucena grabbed hold of his belly as though she were trying to snatch away the child that did not belong to him; to feel through his skin the least sign of movement, of life . . . of love; to communicate to the baby that she was its mother; to bring back the memory of Rodrigo on that day he had made love to her. She seemed as though she were begging forgiveness of this baby she had unknowingly abandoned. Had she known she was pregnant, she never would have given up that body. Never! And now she would give anything, everything, to have the baby in her own womb, to feel it grow, to nurse it, to see it! But it was too late for all that. Now she was in the body of a blind old woman with dried-up breasts and arthritic arms, someone who had nothing to offer the baby but love. Feeling Teo's arm around her shoulder brought Azucena back to reality. She buried her head in his chest, weeping disconsolately. Her sobs blended with those of Ex-Azucena.

"None of you knows what it means for me to have this baby. Don't turn me in. You wouldn't be that cruel. Help me, please, they want to kill me!"

"But why?" asked Azucena, interrupting her own tears. She was concerned now for the future of her child.

"Because you're pregnant?" asked Cuquita.

"No! Don't be silly. That was why they fired me. No, they're going to kill me because that Jezebel doesn't know the meaning of gratitude. Look how she treated me—and after all the years I've slaved for her! What I didn't do for that woman! I anticipated her every whim. I worked thousands of hours overtime. There was no job she gave me that I didn't immediately take care of. . . . Well, there was one I never had the heart for, and that was to kill her daughter."

"That fat girl?" Cuquita interrupted.

"No, the other one, the one she had before her . . . a cute, skinny little thing. How could I ever kill a little baby girl, crazy as I was to have a kid myself. Imagine!"

"So then, who did kill the girl?" asked Azucena.

"No one. I would have liked to have kept her myself, but I couldn't. Working as close to Doña Isabel as I did, sooner or later she would have found out. What could I do! I took her to an orphanage . . ."

The word "orphanage" penetrated Azucena's heart with an icy blast that sent chills up and down her spine. It brought back memories of the cold institution where she had spent her childhood. She shivered, feeling a bond with the poor little girl who, like her, had grown up without a family.

"That's terrible! That must have been one of the most unhappiest satisfactions of your life," remarked Cuquita in her inimitable style.

"Uh, yes," said Ex-Azucena, not really understanding what Cuquita had meant to say.

"But why did Isabel want her killed!" asked Teo, intervening for the first time in the conversation.

"Well, because the little girl's astrological chart said she might topple Isabel from a position of power someday. But me, I think it was pure meanness. I don't know why God gave children to that woman when she never wanted them. You should see how she treats her other daughter, and only because the poor thing's a little heavy."

"Okay, okay, but you still haven't told us why they want to get rid of you," Cuquita insisted.

"Well, because when she told me she didn't want to see me around there a minute more, well, I felt really bad, you know? The witch was tossing me out, and I couldn't swallow that, could I? And so I began thinking about how I'd love to see the lousy bitch changed into a diseased rat, and then have a satellite fall on her and splatter her to kingdom come, and about then, in came one of those head analysts who are always recording what we're thinking, and he told her what was showing up on the screen, and you can imagine how she reacted!"

"But why didn't they kill you then and there!" Cuquita asked, half disappointed that they had let him get away.

"Well, because my buddy Agapito didn't have the nerve. He told the boss that he'd done it, that he'd disintegrated me, but it wasn't true. He hid me in his room until we reached Earth because . . . well, because he sort of likes me, and . . . sort of liked being with me, you know. Then he left me here so I could pray to the Virgin of Guadalupe for help, because he couldn't do anything more for me, but you saw what happened. I didn't even have time to ask for my miracle."

"Hmmm. One thing I'm not clear about. How was it that the photomental camera recorded your real thoughts?" asked Azucena.

"The way it always does, I guess."

"That can't be. My body, I mean, your body, has an implanted microcomputer programmed to emit positive thoughts. With that computer working, it would have been impossible to have photo-mentaled your real thoughts."

"Oh, really? Then maybe the computer you say I got up here failed . . . or had a nervous breakdown . . . I don't know. But whatever it was, Isabel nearly had a stroke."

Azucena, remembering that Dr. Díez had told her that his invention was still in the experimental stages, got excited. That meant that the computer Isabel had in *her* head might act up during the debate that was scheduled to take place within a few hours. What the panel of reporters intended to do during that debate was dig into the candidates' past ten lives, according to the rules of qualification, to see which of the two had the cleanest record. Each one of them, separately, would have to submit to a music-induced regression. Naturally, the reporters had chosen musical themes that would trigger a direct connection with the dark and macabre in the subconscious. If only the apparatus Dr. Díez had fitted Isabel with would fail, as Ex-Azucena's had, Isabel would be revealed to the eyes of the world for the liar she was.

They had to see that debate! It was not something they could afford to miss, but first they had to find Julito, whom they had lost somewhere in the crowd. They finally came across him selling bogus tickets for the purifying waters of El Pocito. Before they had left the building where they had been hiding, Azucena stopped at the door and invited Ex-Azucena to come along with them. Ex-Azucena thanked her profusely.

"Don't thank me. I'm not doing it to be nice, but because I want to be near the man who's going to have my baby."

"Good heavens!" exclaimed Ex-Azucena. He couldn't believe that Azucena's soul was in the body of that little old lady.

"Yes, it's me, and you can get that idiotic look off your face. You didn't kill me, you bastard, just my body, but I'm not going to forget that you tried."

Just as Ex-Azucena was attempting to apologize to Azucena for having killed her, they heard the sound of running feet and ducked into a side street. In silence, they watched as Rodrigo and Citlali ran toward them. Citlali was terrified. Everywhere they'd gone, they'd seen posters with a picture of Citlali's aurograph. She and Rodrigo—more accurately, the body Rodrigo was currently occupying—were accused of being the masterminds behind the plot to assassinate Mr. Bush. As soon as Citlali saw Azucena, Teo, and

Cuquita, she ran to meet them, hugged them warmly, and begged them to help.

"Oh, right," scolded Cuquita. "We look good to you now, huh? But when we needed you, where was your royalty then?"

Azucena prevented the two women from becoming entangled in an endless string of mutual recriminations. She welcomed Rodrigo and Citlali warmly, blessing the "Wanted" posters that had sent the pair running back to them.

Teo's house looked like a substation of the Shrine of Guadalupe. It had, out of necessity, become a sanctuary for everybody. Azucena, Rodrigo, Cuquita, and Julito could not in a million years go back to their apartment building. Citlali's house had been searched by the police, and Ex-Azucena's—besides being watched—had been badly damaged by the earthquake. None of them, as a result, had any choice but to accept Teo's cordial offer. He lived in a small apartment in Tlatelolco. He felt at home in that part of Mexico City, as it had been his haunt in several previous incarnations.

It was the moment for the debate between the two candidates for Planetary President, and all of Teo's guests were sitting around his TV, ready to watch. Like Cuquita, Teo had only a 3-D set, but no one protested. All that interested them was to be able to witness the moment when Isabel made a fool of herself. Azucena was desperate at not being able to see the show. Since Teo was busy preparing dinner for them, Cuquita was charged with narrating to Azucena what was happening, an arrangement that turned out to be a real cross for Azucena. Cuquita couldn't chew gum and report at the same time; she had never been able to do two things simultaneously, so now she was either watching the screen or telling what had happened. She would become entranced by the interesting parts and her tongue would freeze while she gaped at the images. All Azucena could do was listen to the music being played during the regression and repeatedly ask Cuquita what was happening on the screen.

Azucena didn't have much of a choice. Rodrigo and Citlali were hugging and smooching at every opportunity and had no time for anything besides themselves. Ex-Azucena was a disaster; he freely embellished the picture, narrating more than he actually saw, and there was no way to shut him up once he began talking. Julito was already half drunk, and kept making stupid remarks, so Azucena's only option was Cuquita, however hopeless she seemed.

It was bad enough that she would suddenly fall silent; but in addition, she dozed during the boring parts, so that Azucena didn't know whether what was happening was incredibly interesting or incredibly dull. Right then, however, things were definitely dull. The European candidate's most recent ten lives were the most boring anyone could imagine. Cuquita had fallen into such a deep sleep that she wasn't even snoring. Azucena hated the silence, it left her in total darkness. She needed the sound of a voice in order to connect to the present, otherwise, her senses were left at the mercy of the same music the presidential candidates were hearing, and her mind would begin to wander. She became lost in the blackness to which she was condemned and ended up traveling through her own past lives. There was nothing terrible about that, but it wasn't what she wanted. She wanted to be the first to know whether or not Isabel's computer would fail her.

When Isabel's turn came to be regressed, the silence in the room was absolute. All of them had their fingers crossed, hoping the implanted computer would malfunction. Isabel's first three lives were reviewed without incident. Her problems began when they came to her life as Mother Teresa. At first it went very well. Images of her life as a saint appeared on the screen in meticulous detail. She was shown carrying an undernourished child in Ethiopia, distributing food among lepers, but then . . . the microcomputer finally fizzled out!

CD
Track 9

Rodrigo yelled, "That's my regression! That woman was me!"

Upon hearing this, Azucena was startled back to the present from where she had been wandering in memory. The silence of Cuquita, as well as the others, had left her at the mercy of the music and she herself had slipped into regression—not too far into the past, only to the beginning of her present lifetime. She learned that it had been an extremely difficult birth. The umbilical cord had been wrapped three times around her neck. Three times! She had barely escaped being stillborn. The doctors had revived her, but she had come very close to succeeding in strangling herself. And the reason she had wanted to kill herself was that she knew her mother was going to be none other than Isabel González. What a nightmare! And *she* was that daughter Isabel had ordered killed! To add to the complications, Ex-Azucena, the bodyguard she held such a grudge against for having killed her body and claimed it for his own, was the person who had saved her life when she was a baby. It seemed that on the one hand she owed him her life; and on the other hand, her death.

Rodrigo's shouting once again startled her from her thoughts.

"Azucena! Did you hear me? Isabel's life is the same one *I* saw!"

Azucena was so stunned by what she had just discovered about herself that it took a while to realize what Rodrigo—aided, of course, by that busybody Cuquita—was trying to tell her: that Isabel was a murderer of the worst kind, that in one lifetime she had impaled people, that in another she had stabbed and killed Rodrigo's brother-in-law, and that now everything was going to come out in the open, that she'd been hogtied and humiliated in front of the entire population of the planet, that she deserved it for being such a monster, that she was sure to be killed for having deceived everybody with the microcomputer she had implanted in her head, that it was only a matter of time until they themselves were going to be exonerated completely, and on and on.

That pipe dream ended when Teo made everyone quiet down and watch what was happening. The television screen was blank. An announcement was being made to viewers explaining that the station was experiencing technical difficulties. Abel Zabludowsky was reading a special bulletin from the Planetary Attorney General's office, informing the public of reported sabotage. In sum, what they were attempting to do was to convince viewers that the images they had just seen were faked, that they were transmitted by saboteurs who had taken over the Televirtual studio and whose objective was to smear Isabel.

"No!" they all shouted. "We saw it with our own eyes!"

Azucena was desperate. They had to prove somehow that Isabel was a liar. It was the only way to defeat her. Julito quickly began taking bets on whether or not they'd succeed. The pessimists among them were inclined toward failure, but not Azucena. She could not give up. She was ready to go to the final round, to do whatever it took to win, even if that meant all-out war. But it wasn't that simple. On Earth, no one had weapons. She and Julito had a plan to organize a guerrilla force, but to carry it off they needed money, contacts, and a spacecraft for transporting the arms—and they had none of those things.

The most direct action they could manage would be to present proof that the images the entire world had seen were authentic. They had to get their hands on them. But where? If only they still had the cybernetic Ouija! They'd had to leave it in Julito's spaceship, and the ship itself had been left behind on a very distant planet. Well, no use crying over that. They'd had no choice. Even worse was that, in leaving Azucena's apartment so abruptly, they'd lost the photos of Rodrigo's regression, the compact disc, the Discman, the African violet with its information, and all the photographs relating to the murder of Dr. Díez. And they had no way of recovering any of it.

Azucena didn't know where to begin. She went to look for Teo, and put her arms around him. She wanted him to flood her with peace. She was so exhausted from thinking, that she let her mind go blank, and, as she did, the diamond in her forehead filled her with Divine Light. She experienced a moment of incredible lucidity. She remembered that during the regression she had guided Rodrigo through on the spaceship, she had learned from him that Citlali, the Indian he had raped in 1521, had raped him in 1890, during his life as a woman. If the male Citlali was the brother-in-law who had raped Rodrigo, then she'd been Isabel's brother. And therefore, if they could perform a regression with Citlali, they would have access to the scene where Isabel the husband murdered Citlali, his brother.

It was exasperating not to have the music they needed at hand. Azucena tried to console herself by thinking that even if they could perform the regression and get new photomentals, the images wouldn't help in any case, since they couldn't very well take them to the police while they themselves were being sought. They'd have to get new proof somewhere else.

Citlali remembered that she still had the spoon Azucena had been so interested in at the flea market. Azucena brightened a moment, but her spirits fell once again as she realized that they didn't have the cybernetic Ouija to test it. It would have been extremely helpful to obtain an analysis of the spoon. Azucena remembered that in one of the photos in Rodrigo's regression the face of the rapist was reflected in the spoon, along with the face of the person who had stolen up behind him to stab him in the back—that is, the face of Isabel in her male incarnation. That would surely be convincing evidence to incriminate our sweet candidate!

What a nuisance not to be able to obtain that image! Cuquita suggested that they try to perform a regression on the spoon.

Everyone laughed at her but Azucena, who thought her suggestion made a lot of sense. All objects vibrate and are susceptible to music, possessing the additional advantage of not being afflicted with the emotional blocks that hamper human beings. But the plan was still stymied because they had no music to set the spoon vibrating, nor a photomental camera to register the memories. Cuquita came to the rescue, offering to sing a favorite *danzón*. She said she didn't need any accompaniment. So Teo pulled out a beat-up old photomental camera from a closet and everyone concentrated together to make the experiment work.

Rodrigo was to hold the spoon in his hand to activate memories of the life they wanted to revisit. And Cuquita, with absolute self-assurance, began to belt out the lyrics of "At Your Mercy," at the top of her lungs.

Intermission for Dancing

CD
Track 10

For everyone who enjoys
Vegetables and fruits
Comes this danzón *dedicated*
To Your Mercy Marketplace.

The mangoes all were chatting about how
The limes were so fresh,
And how the ordinary orange
Thinks she's such a tangerine.
And the prickly pears, led on
By the two-faced apple,
Grabbed the poor olives
For a midday snack.
Everything passes, everything passes,
Even . . . the prune passes.

Señoras, don't be so petty,
For all of us are tasty enough.
Some think they're fancy currants
But are only sour grapes.
"Ooh, what grand neighbors I have,"
Mocked the dark-skinned sapodilla,
Who later criticized the quince
For looking like a yellow gringo.
"Don't be so vulgar,"
Replied the pomegranate,
"You're just a swarthy sapodilla
And no one said anything to you."
Everything passes, everything passes,
Even . . . the prune passes.

LILIANA FELIPE

Cuquita lapped up the thunderous, ego-stroking applause. Her voice, more jolting than ammonia, shook out of the spoon every last drop of its rape scene. The fugitives were very pleased with themselves. The images were clear, although the reflections in the spoon were small and difficult to see. Teo had to go to his computer to make enlargements. Among them, he obtained a perfect reproduction of the male Isabel's face at the very moment she was murdering her brother, the male Citlali. But despite this, they could still not say that their problems were solved.

What they had was evidence that proved to them they were correct in their suppositions, but a good lawyer would discredit that photo in a second if they offered it as proof of Isabel's guilt. He could say, yes, that probably was the face of the murderer, but the photo in no way proved conclusively that the murderer was Isabel. And he would be correct, because the images revealed to the world on Televirtual as a part of Isabel's regression showed the scene not in the reflection in the spoon but from a different perspective: the murderer's, and in those images the killer was never seen. The fact that the crime was viewed through the murderer's eyes meant that his face was at no time visible, and therefore a photograph of it, though authentic, could not serve to implicate Isabel. The defense could allege that the image in the spoon had been computer enhanced. It was a shame, because the photograph was so good.

Azucena was totally frustrated that she herself could not examine the photo. Her only recourse was to recreate in her mind the description Rodrigo gave her. As she began visualizing it, Azucena felt as if she were close to retrieving some forgotten fact. Suddenly, she cried out: "I have it!" According to what Rodrigo had told her, Citlali's male face appeared in the foreground of the reflection in the spoon. In the middle distance was Isabel's male face. And in the background was the upper portion of a stained glass window. Azucena's pulse began beating more rapidly. The description of the stained glass was identical to that of the window she had watched fall toward her in 1985. The scene of the earthquake flashed before her mind with the same intensity she had felt the first time she'd viewed it. In a flash she again witnessed Rodrigo picking her up in his arms; saw the ceiling falling toward them; again experienced the confusion, pain, silence, dust, blood, debris; saw the legs of someone walking over to where she lay; and the hands lifting a stone that in an instant would thud down upon her head . . . and in the split second before the impact, she saw the hatred on Isabel's face. She remembered that at the precise moment she had turned her head, trying to avoid being crushed by the stone, and . . . her mind stopped, a blank. Her recollections froze into a single image: just before she died, as she turned away, her eyes—she was sure of it!—had caught a glimpse of the Pyramid of Love buried beneath the rubble of the house. Engraved in her mind was the scene in which Rodrigo had raped Citlali. Her mental masturbations had made her return to it again and again, but now she remembered that Rodrigo had told her that he'd raped Citlali on the Temple of Love. That was the same pyramid she had seen beneath her house as she died. So all she had to do was find out the exact location of the house and look for the Pyramid.

As long as she was having no luck in rejoining her twin soul, at least she could fulfill her mission in life. Azucena asked Teo to help her and quickly got to work. With the help of a pendulum and a map, she soon pinpointed the address of the house. Ex-Azucena nearly choked when he heard it—that was Isabel's address! This complicated everything. Ex-Azucena confirmed that in fact a pyramid had long been struggling to break through the patio of that house. Azucena realized they were in real trouble for sure now, because Isabel's house was an impregnable fortress and none of them could possibly gain entry. Ex-Azucena, however, gave them heart. He knew a way to get into the fortress, and that was through Carmela, Azucena's sister, Isabel's fat daughter. Carmela truly loved Ex-Azucena. He was the only person who had shown her any affection during her childhood, staying by her side when she was ill, helping her with homework, bringing her flowers on her birthday, taking her out Sunday afternoons, telling her she was pretty, and never neglecting to kiss her good night. He was absolutely sure, therefore, that if he asked her for help, she would not refuse him, because she had been like a daughter to him.

"And besides," he said, "she won't care if we're using her help to get at Isabel, because the truth is, she never loved her mother. The hatred between them has always been mutual."

Teo commented that it was precisely the smoldering resentment generated by such relationships that had given rise to revolutions throughout history. At any given moment, the outcasts, the forgotten, the mistreated banded together against the powerful. The sad part was that once the downtrodden had triumphed and replaced those in power, their only thought was revenge and they ended up being no better than the ones they'd unseated—until, in turn, a new group of malcontents seized power from them. That, unfortunately, was the way things went. Only when they are the oppressed do people see injustice for what it is. When they are in a position of power, they will rule without mercy, resorting to anything to avoid losing the throne.

It is extremely difficult to pass the test of power. Most people become possessed by demons, forgetting everything they've learned as one of the powerless and committing all manner of atrocities. The solution for humanity will come only on that day when those who assume power do so by acting in accordance with the Law of Love. Azucena was convinced that this would happen only at the moment when the Pyramid was restored to its proper function. All the others were in agreement with her, and so they resolved to get in contact with Carmela.

Unfortunately, at that very moment, just as they were nearing the point of solving their problem, just when they had all the necessary information at hand, the police arrived to arrest them.

16

No holds were barred during the trial of Isabel González. The Law of Love was at stake. Anacreonte advised Azucena, while Mammon defended Isabel. Nergal, chief of Hell's secret police, was special counsel to the defense, and the Archangel Michael, to the prosecutors. Devils and cherubim alike looked after the jurors. Mammon prayed. Anacreonte cursed. And they all tried every dirty trick in the book. The battle was bloody: only the strongest would survive. But it was impossible to predict the outcome. From the very beginning it was obvious that both sides had an equal chance at victory.

Isabel had trained hard. Since she knew she had to fight a clean fight, that is, without the aid of a microcomputer, she had enlisted the help of a shady guru. Well aware that the jury would be composed primarily of mediums, Isabel reasoned that to convince them of her innocence it was imperative that she master— by sheer willpower—the images her mind emitted. After months of intense training, she was able to impede her true thoughts and to project, strongly and clearly, whatever images she chose to have others observe. She had become extremely skillful in preventing mediums from gaining entry to her private thoughts. They were thoroughly perplexed. They did not trust her, yet they could find nothing false in her testimony. Thus in plain view Isabel managed to inflict a series of low blows, without anyone's realizing it.

ROUND ONE
Right Cross!

The first to come forward to testify on behalf of the defense had been Ricardo Rodríguez, Cuquita's husband. The dummy had accepted a bribe in return for confessing to Mr. Bush's murder. Isabel had promised him that as soon as she won her case and ascended to power, she would pardon him. Ricardo Rodríguez took her at her word, convinced he'd end up living like a king for the rest of his days. What he didn't know was that Isabel's word meant nothing, and that she couldn't have cared less about helping him. Ricardo had fastened the noose around his own neck and, in the process, entangled Cuquita, Azucena, Rodrigo, Citlali, Teo, and Julito, by accusing them of being his accomplices.

ROUND TWO
Jab to the Kidneys!

The prosecution answered that first blow with testimony from Ex-Azucena, who explained in minute detail his participation in the murders of Mr. Bush, Azucena, and Dr. Díez. He related how each had been killed and accused Isabel of being the mastermind. The jury was clearly moved, not only by the sincerity of his statements but by the angelic appearance of a woman nine months pregnant.

ROUND THREE
Below the Belt!

To counter the positive effect of Ex-Azucena's testimony, the defense called Agapito to the stand. Agapito claimed that while it was true Ex-Azucena had been involved with him in all the murders, Ex-Azucena had acted on his, Agapito's, orders—not Isabel's. He declared himself to be the mastermind of all the crimes, absolving Isabel of all responsibility. He stated that he alone had planned the murders. He could not provide a convincing motive for having committed the crimes, but the one fact he emphasized over and over was that he had acted completely on his own. Isabel gained a lot of ground with this testimony.

ROUND FOUR
Left Jab!

As the next witness, the prosecutor called Cuquita, but the lawyer for the defense attempted to disqualify her from testifying. Her past life as a film critic made her a witness of dubious credibility. It was not that she'd been a critic per se, but rather that her sole motivation as such had been envy. Innumerable venomous reviews had flowed from her pen. She had maliciously meddled in the private lives of everyone she wrote about. The few times she had written anything favorable, it had been merely the result of cronyism, never impartial analysis. Furthermore, in her curriculum vitae there was no evidence to show that she'd ever repaid that karma.

Cuquita claimed over and over that she had done so by living with her husband, who was a royal pain in the ass, but the defense lawyer countered that assertion with depositions that characterized Ricardo Rodríguez in highly favorable terms, referring to him as a saint and stating that the one with the checkered past was Cuquita. Cuquita was furious, but there was nothing she could do.

What annoyed her more than anything was that she had missed her opportunity to perform before the Televirtual cameras. All her life she had been preparing for the possibility that one day she would be a witness to a crime. In every trip she made to the market, she tried to memorize the features of all the customers, in case later she would need to describe one of them to the police. Or she would attempt to remember every detail of her expedition: how many people were at the vegetable stands, how many oranges her neighbor had bought, what denominations of coins she'd used to pay, whether she'd haggled with the vendor over the price, whether the vendor had threatened her with a knife. And that wasn't all.

Her tabloid mind-set made her think about the remote chance that she might end up as the victim rather than the witness, so she also prepared for that eventuality. She never left home with a hole in her underwear or stockings. She was terrified by the possibility that she'd be taken to the hospital, and the doctors, removing her outer clothing, would discover how slovenly she was. And now, all that preparation down the drain!

ROUND FIVE
Jolting Hook to the Kidneys!

The prosecutor, set back by the dismissal of his previous witness, called Citlali to the stand. Her testimony could prove damaging. While serving her sentence in the prison rehabilitation program, she had had more than enough time to work through her past lives. It had become very clear to her just what her connections to Isabel had been. Citlali began her testimony by recounting her life in 1521. In that incarnation, Citlali had murdered Isabel's newborn baby, and Isabel had died hating her. In their next parallel lives, Isabel and she had been brothers. Citlali had raped her brother's wife, and, in return, Isabel had murdered her.

Then the Law of Love had come into play to balance the relationship between them, causing them to be born as mother and daughter, to see whether those ties could ease the hatred Citlali felt for Isabel. All in vain. Isabel had never loved her daughter. She more or less tolerated her as a little girl, but as soon as Citlali reached adolescence, Isabel perceived her as an enemy. Isabel had been divorced in that life. As the years went by, she had met Rodrigo and had fallen in love with him. They had married when Citlali was still a girl, but when Citlali began to turn into a young woman, Rodrigo, to Isabel's horror, had begun looking at her with different eyes. Finally, the day came when what Isabel most feared happened. Rodrigo and Citlali ran away from Isabel's home and became lovers.

Isabel found them living in a run-down old mansion in the center of the city. Citlali was pregnant and madly in love. Isabel was furious. Jealousy drove her over the edge. The day of the earthquake in 1985, she had run to where the lovers lived, not to see if her daughter Citlali was still alive but because she wanted to know whether Rodrigo had survived the earthquake. She had found them both dead, but beneath the rubble she discovered Azucena—who in that life was her granddaughter—alive. Blind with hatred, she had crushed the infant's head with a stone.

ROUND SIX
Below the Belt!

Citlali's testimony had hurt Isabel but, as always, when it seemed she was down for the count, the defense attorney turned things around 180 degrees and seemed to make the facts favor Isabel.

First, he asked Citlali what proof she had to substantiate her testimony. Citlali had none. The reason was that several years back Isabel had tracked her down, taking advantage of a moment when Citlali was in the hospital, to program her mind so that Citlali would never remember the lives in which she witnessed Isabel's crimes. Who knows what techniques they had used in the rehabilitation program to allow her access to those lives; but the fact was that while she was able to gain entry into those memories, her mind was unable to project them as evidence, because Isabel had put a block on her ability to project images. The only person who knew the password to override that program was Isabel herself, and it would be a cold day in hell before she'd let that out. So Citlali's testimony ended up having about as much impact as a leaf in a storm.

In addition, the defense attorney insisted that in 1985 Isabel was not Isabel, but Mother Teresa. He reminded the jury that Isabel was a former saint who had achieved a very high degree of evolution and was absolutely truthful. He asked them to look her in the eye and satisfy themselves that she was innocent of the crimes she was charged with.

Isabel withstood the penetrating gaze of mediums without flinching. The jury could not detect the least sign of deception in her eyes. Isabel smiled. Everything was working out just as she'd planned. She was certain that no one would be able to prove anything against her. Immediately after the presidential debate, she had had the microcomputer removed from her head, and there was no proof she'd ever had one. She had ordered her house to be dynamited, to avoid the possibility of having its walls analyzed. They would have provided damning evidence. Fortunately for her, no trace of them remained.

The only thing she hadn't fully managed to control was the extent of the explosion. It had uncovered the pyramid in her patio. But that hadn't been much of a problem. Before the police arrived to investigate the apparent assassination attempt against her, she had had time to remove the apex of the Pyramid of Love from the rubble. This stone had been her only remaining concern. She had taken it to the shrine of Our Lady of Guadalupe, and dropped it into the waters of El Pocito. She felt sure that no one would ever find it again. As long as the Temple of Love was not functioning, people would concentrate their love on themselves, not being able to see beyond their own image in the water's reflection. There was no better place to hide it. It would never be found, and therefore no one could use it to prove her culpability. She felt calm and collected. The rose quartz stone she had used to murder Azucena in 1985 was certainly not about to float.

Carmela was next to give testimony as a witness for the defense. She was truly unrecognizable. The time that had passed since her mother's presidential debate had completely transformed her. The principal reason was that Carmela had met her sister, Azucena, and that had given Carmela a different view of the world. The meeting between the two had turned out to be more beneficial than anyone would have imagined. They had come to love each other so much that Carmela, from the pure pleasure of being accepted and appreciated, had lost five hundred and twenty-eight pounds.

The first meeting between the two had taken place in the visitors' room of the José López Guido Rehabilitation Facility. Azucena had been sentenced to spend several months there. Those months turned out to be the most pleasant of her entire life, since the first thing prison officials did with new inmates was give them an examination to determine how much rejection and love privation had accumulated in their hearts. Using that information as a base, a plan was elaborated to replace any and all lack of love, because the staff was aware that the absence of love is the source of criminal behavior, fault finding, aggression, and resentment.

Azucena did not suffer through her sentence; she enjoyed it. At this institution, the greater the lack of love in one's past lives, the greater the coddling one received as treatment. For it was through love and attention that criminals were reintegrated into society. Of course, if it was discovered during the examination that a criminal had not actually been deprived of love but had acted under a Demon's influence, then that person was sent to the Alphonse Capone Memorial Pavilion at Negro Durazo Prison, where they specialized in performing exorcisms.

This was in fact what had happened to Julito. They had sent him to prison there, arguing that he was possessed by the Devil, and that "an enormous arsenal of explosives" had been uncovered in his house. Nothing of the sort: the "arsenal" actually consisted of some fireworks Julito used in his Interplanetary Cockfight productions; but since there was no way he could convince the authorities of his innocence, he was carted off to the Pavilion. Rodrigo, Cuquita, Ex-Azucena, Citlali, and Teo, like Azucena, had been remanded to the López Guido rehab facility, but finally all of them, even their old pal Julito, did marvelously.

Both institutions included first-rate astroanalysts among their staff. Rodrigo had even begun the process of recovering his memory. Having Citlali with him was extremely beneficial. They had been installed in a matrimonial suite. There, between orgasms, his past was coming to light. Of course, he had made no progress in remembering the lives in which he'd witnessed Isabel's crimes. The astroanalysts did not have the correct password, and without it, they could never gain full access to his subconscious. Rodrigo knew that Isabel was the only person who had the key. But how to get it out of her? Isabel gave every sign of being invincible.

ROUND SEVEN
Staggering Blow to the Head!

Isabel knew she was winning the battle, and was calmly awaiting
Carmela's testimony. Thank God the girl has lost weight, she
thought. She no longer had to be embarrassed by her. Carmela
looked quite lovely now, and provoked a lot of admiring glances.
Isabel felt extremely proud of her daughter, and was even beginning to like her.

"What is your name?"

"Carmela González."

"What is your relationship to the accused?"

"I'm her daughter."

"How long have you lived with your mother?"

"Eighteen years."

"And during that time, have you ever known her to lie?"

"Yes."

A murmur rippled through the courtroom. Isabel's mouth tight-
ened. The defense attorney was thrown completely off guard.
This had not been in his plans.

"And on what occasion?"

"There were many."

"Could you be more specific? Give us an example."

"Certainly. She told me I was her only daughter."

"And isn't that the case?"

"No. I have a sister."

The defense attorney glanced at Isabel. He knew nothing about
this information, but he didn't like the smell of it. This could turn
out to be dangerous. Isabel's jaw had dropped. She couldn't imagine where Carmela had obtained that information.

"Why do you say that?"

"Rosalío Chávez told me."

"The bodyguard your mother recently dismissed?"

"Yes, that's the one."

"And you trusted information given you by a person who obviously was resentful for having been dismissed?"

"Objection!" shouted the prosecutor.

"Sustained," ruled the judge.

So Carmela did not have to answer the question. The defense attorney wiped his brow. He had no idea how to extricate himself from the mess he'd stumbled into.

"And do you think that this Mr. Rosalío Chávez is a person who can be trusted?"

"Not only that, I consider him my true mother."

Exclamations of surprise reverberated throughout the courtroom. Ex-Azucena wept with emotion. He had never expected such public recognition of his role as substitute mother. Isabel's composure was crumbling by the minute. Fucking little fat-ass, you'll pay for this! she thought. Isabel motioned to her attorney, who hurried over to confer with her. Isabel whispered a few words into his ear, and the attorney returned to the witness with a telling question on his lips.

"Is it true that you've suffered all your life from obesity?"

"Yes, that's true."

"And isn't it true that this problem caused many arguments and confrontations with your mother?"

"Yes, that's true."

"And isn't it true that you envied your mother terribly because she could eat anything she wanted without putting on weight?"

"That's correct."

"And isn't it also true that for this reason you determined to take your revenge by coming here to this court to testify against her, even though you have no way of proving what you say?"

"Objection!" cried the prosecutor.

"Sustained," said the judge.

Carmela realized that once again she did not have to respond to the question, but this time she wanted to do so.

"Your Honor, I'd like to answer that question. May I?"

"Go ahead."

"For one thing, what motivated me to testify is a desire to see justice done. I no longer have anything to envy, because now, as all of you can see, I'm thinner than she is. And I *do* have a way of proving the things I've said." Removing a piece of leaded glass from her handbag, Carmela handed it to the judge. "If I may, I'd like to present this piece of stained glass as evidence. If you have it analyzed you'll see that I'm not lying."

Carmela had been extremely clever. First, in managing to remove a section of stained glass from the window, as Ex-Azucena had asked, before Isabel had the house dynamited; and second, in presenting it as proof that Isabel had lied to her about the existence of her sister. To obtain images of the events the glass had witnessed, the court ordered a complete analysis of its history, from the day it was made up until the present.

In the course of that analysis, Isabel's crimes were revealed, one by one. The first to come to light was what had happened in 1890. From its vantage point, the stained glass had witnessed the male Isabel creep into the room where the male Citlali was raping the female Rodrigo, and offered a clear image of Isabel plunging the knife into Citlali's back. This image corresponded perfectly to the one that viewers around the world had seen on the day of the debate, the only discrepancy being merely that the scene was witnessed from a different perspective. Farther on, images of the 1985 crime against Azucena appeared. These shots were blurred since, like everything else in the house, the stained glass window was vibrating from the earthquake. From its high perspective, however, it had witnessed the moment Rodrigo ran into the bedroom and picked up his daughter. But before he could escape with her, a beam fell on him, killing him. And then there was dust and darkness. The next image showed Isabel entering the room to find Rodrigo and Citlali dead in the rubble. Next her attention was drawn to the crying baby. Isabel walked over to her and saw that she was unharmed. Then with both hands she lifted up a large stone of rose quartz and smashed it down brutally upon the little head. The image showed in excruciating detail the icy emotions on Isabel's face at that moment, when she looked just a few years younger than in her present life. No one could deny that Isabel was indeed the one who had murdered that baby!

Finally came images of Isabel in 2180, with a baby in her arms. Waiting for her in the room was Rosalío Chávez as he appeared before he'd obtained Azucena's body. Isabel handed him the little girl and ordered him to disintegrate her for one hundred years. Taking the child in his arms, Rosalío left the room.

ROUND EIGHT
Knockout!

Isabel was finished. The defense had run out of arguments. The prosecutor asked the judge's permission to question Azucena Martínez, explaining that Azucena was the girl Isabel had ordered killed but, fortunately, she had survived. She was now here to offer her testimony. The judge agreed. Azucena was led into the courtroom. Before reaching the witness stand, she paused as Carmela gave her an affectionate hug.

Isabel felt her strength draining from her. Her daughter was alive! So she had not prevailed over fate. Her teeth chattered like castanets. She heard disgrace knocking at her door and went numb with fear. She could not absorb the turn of events and did not want to see any more of what was going on. But curiosity made her turn to look at her daughter Azucena for the first time. She found it impossible to believe that the aged woman who had just entered the courtroom was her daughter. What was going on? Azucena was sworn in. The prosecutor began his questioning.

"What is your name?"

"Azucena Martínez."

"What is your profession?"

"I am an astroanalyst."

"That means that you're continually involved with other people's past lives, is that true?"

"Yes."

"Did you ever wish you had experienced some part of your patients' lives?"

"Objection!" shouted the defense attorney.

"Overruled," declared the judge.

"Yes."

"Could you tell us when that was?"

"Yes. Whenever they had lived a happy childhood with their mother."

"Why was that?"

"Because my mother abandoned me when I was a baby. I never knew her."

"And if you had ever met her, would you have complained to her about how she'd abandoned you?"

"I would have, before I served my term at the rehabilitation facility."

"And how did your stay there change your way of thinking?"

"I not only forgave my mother for having abandoned me, but also for twice trying to have me killed."

Azucena looked in Isabel's direction, her blind eyes shining brightly. Isabel shuddered at the intensity of her gaze. Azucena was telling the truth. There was no hatred in her. No one had ever gazed on Isabel with love. Everyone around her regarded her with fear, respect, or mistrust—never with love. Isabel could not take any more, and burst into tears. Her days of villainy were over.

"I promise to abide by and to enforce the Law of Love from this day forward." Much against her will, Isabel had to speak those words, at which time her trial was declared ended. As part of her sentence, she had been named Consul in Korma. Her one mission from now on would be to teach the Kormian natives to understand the Law of Love.

Her words affected no one more greatly than Rodrigo and Citlali. The password to their memories was precisely the word "love," spoken by Isabel. When Rodrigo heard it, he felt like Noah, on the day the rains ceased. The oppression weighing on his mind vanished. The constant feeling that there was something he was supposed to put back where it belonged disappeared. He breathed a deep sigh and felt a profound sense of peace. His eyes fixed upon Azucena's, and light glowed between them. He immediately recognized her as his twin soul. They relived their first meeting in its entirety, except that this time they had an audience. When the music of the spheres faded, Rodrigo, inflamed with love, asked Azucena to marry him that very day. All their friends accompanied them to the shrine of Guadalupe. The first thing they did there was visit El Pocito to perform the rite. And the moment Rodrigo leaned over to take some water, he spotted the capstone to the Pyramid of Love.

The notes of a distant conch sounded as they set the rose quartz stone in place. The air was replete with the aroma of warm tortillas and newly baked bread. The city of Gran Tenochtitlán appeared before them and, superimposed on it, colonial Mexico City. Then, in a unique phenomenon, the two cities became fused.

The voices of Nahua poets chanted in unison with those of Spanish monks. The eyes of all present were able to look deep into the eyes of any other, without apprehension. No barrier existed. The other person was oneself. For a moment, all hearts harbored Divine Love equally. Everyone felt part of a whole. Love struck them like lightning, penetrating every space in their bodies. At times the flesh could not contain it, and its truth burst out in a tingling on the skin. As Cuquita said, it was an "awe-expiring" spectacle.

CD
Track 11

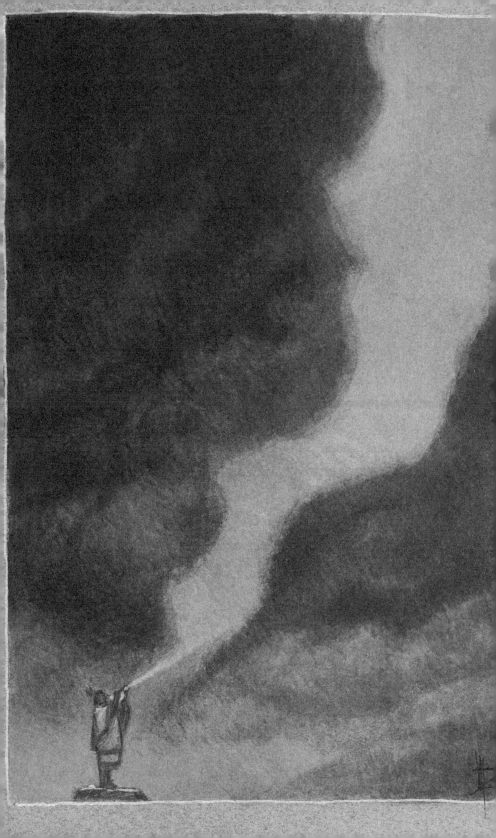

Like a mighty hurricane, love erased every vestige of rancor, of hatred. No one could remember why they'd ever grown apart from a loved one. The reincarnated Hugo Sánchez forgot that it was Dr. Mejía Barón who had not allowed him to play in the 1994 soccer World Cup. Cuquita forgot the beatings her husband had given her all those years. Carmela forgot that Isabel always called her a pig. Julito forgot that he liked only women with fat asses. Cats forgot that they despised mice. The Palestinians forgot their bitterness toward the Jews. Suddenly there were no more racists or torturers. Bodies forgot knife wounds, bullet wounds, gashes, kicks, torture, blows, and opened their pores to caresses and kisses. Tear ducts prepared to shed tears of joy; throats to sob with pleasure; mouth muscles to trace the broadest of smiles; heart muscles to expand and expand until they gave birth to pure love. Just like Ex-Azucena's womb.

His time had come. In the midst of the cacophony of love, he gave birth to a beautiful baby girl. She was born without a moment's pain, in absolute harmony. She came into a world that welcomed her with open arms and so had no reason to cry. Nor Ex-Azucena to remain on Earth: with the birth, his mission was fulfilled. Lovingly, he bid his daughter good-bye and died with a wink of his eye.

Rodrigo gave the baby to Azucena and she hugged her tenderly. She could not see her baby, but she knew exactly what she was like. Azucena wished with all her heart and soul to have a young body so that she could care for the child. The Gods took pity on her, allowing her to occupy her former body once again as a reward for all her efforts in carrying out her mission.

As soon as Azucena reentered her body, Anacreonte's mission was complete. He was at total liberty to go off and enjoy his honeymoon. During the trial, he had courted Pavana, and they had just been married. As for Lilith, she had married Mammon.

Within a few months, the former couple had a cuddly little cherub, and the latter, a dimpled little demon.

On Earth, all was happiness. Citlali had found her twin soul. Cuquita had found hers. Teo was promoted. Carmela discovered that she was hopelessly in love with Julito and they were married without delay. Order finally had been reestablished and all doubts resolved. Azucena learned that she had been assigned the mission of reinstating the Law of Love as part of a punishment. She had been the most foul murderer of all time, having blown up three planets with nuclear bombs. But the Law of Love, in its infinite generosity, had given her the opportunity to restore equilibrium. And to the benefit of all, she had succeeded.

I perceive the secret, the hidden,
O you, our lords!
Thus we are:
We are mortals,
And four by four we mortals
All must go away,
All must die on earth . . .
Like a painting, we shall go on fading.
Like a flower,
We shall wither
Here upon the earth.
Like the vestment of the zacuán,
Of the precious bird with the collar of blood,
We shall go on ending . . .

Think upon this, O lords:
Eagles and tigers,
Were you made of jade,
Were you made of gold,
There still would you go,
To the place of the uncarnate.
We must all disappear,
No one is to remain.

"Romances de los Señores de Nueva
España," fol. 36 r.
NEZAHUALCÓYOTL
Trece Poetas del Mundo Azteca
MIGUEL LEÓN-PORTILLA

CONTENTS OF CD

1. Vogliatemi Bene (Dueto de amor)/frag.**   3:02
   Madam Butterfly / G. Puccini (Casa Ricordi BMG S.p.A.)

2. Mala   3:27
   (Liliana Felipe/Ed. El Hábito)

3. Burundanga   2:14
   (O. Bouffartique/EMI)

4. O Mio Babbino Caro*   2:33
   Gianni Schicchi/G. Puccini (Casa Ricordi BMG S.p.A.)

5. Nessun Dorma*   2:47
   Turandot/G. Puccini (Casa Ricordi BMG S.p.A.)

6. A Nadie   3:36
   (Liliana Felipe/Ed. El Hábito)

7. Senza Mamma (frag.)**   2:49
   Suor Angelica/G. Puccini (Casa Ricordi BMG S.p.A.)

8. San Miguel Arcángel   5:15
   (Liliana Felipe/Ed. El Hábito)

9. Tre Sbirri. Una Carrozza. (frag.)*   3:42
   Tosca/G. Puccini (Casa Ricordi BMG S.p.A.)

10. A Su Merced   6:26
    (Liliana Felipe/Ed. El Hábito)

11. Finale**   2:13
    Finale: Saludo Caracolas—Quetzalcoatl, 4 elementos
    Canto Cardenche; Versos de Pastorela (frag.)
    "Diecimila anni al nostro Imperatore!" (frag.)
    Turandot/G. Puccini (Casa Ricordi BMG S.p.A.)

MUSIC CREDITS

WORKS OF GIACOMO PUCCINI

SOPRANO: REGINA OROZCO
TENOR: ARMANDO MORA

ORQUESTA DE BAJA CALIFORNIA
CONDUCTOR: EDUARDO GARCÍA BARRIOS

ORCHESTRATION: SERGIO RAMÍREZ*/DMITRI DUDIN**
ARTISTIC AND MUSICAL DIRECTION: EDUARDO GARCÍA BARRIOS

Concert Master: Igor Tchetchko
First Violins: Tatiana Freedland
Alyze Drelling
Second Violins: Jean Young
Heather Frank
Viola I: Sara Mullen
Viola II: Cynthia Saye
Cello: Omar Firestone
Double bass: Dean Ferrell
Flute: Sebastian Winston
Oboe: Boris Glouzman
Clarinet I: Vladimir Goltsman
Clarinet II: Alexandr Gurievich
Bassoon: Pavel Getman
French horn: Jane Zwerneman
Trumpet: Joe Dyke
Trombone: Loren Marsteller
Piano: Olena Getman
Harp: Elena Mashkovtseva
Percussion I: Andrei Thernishev
Percussion II: Alan Silverstein

Guest artists on *Senza Mamma:*
Viola II: Paula Simmons
Cello II: Renata Bratts

Chorus: Unidad Cristiana de México A.R.
and members of the choral workshop of the Orquesta de Baja California

Guest soloist: Laura Sosa

Conches and *tarahumera* drum: Ana Luisa Solís

Recording engineers: Luis Gil and Sergio Ramírez
Assistant engineer: Luis Cortés
Production assistant: Renata Ramos
Recorded in Tijuana B.C. in Autumn 1995

DANZONES

COMPOSER AND LEAD SINGER: LILIANA FELIPE

ORCHESTRA: DANZONERA DIMAS
CONDUCTOR: FELIPE PÉREZ
ARRANGEMENTS: LILIANA FELIPE AND DMITRI DUDIN

Tenor saxophone: Amador Pérez
Alto saxophone/clarinet II: Félix Guillén
Alto saxophone/clarinet I: Andrés Martínez
Alto saxophone/clarinet III: Eloy López
Trumpet III: Felipe Castillo
Trumpet II: Pepe Millar
Trumpet I: Abel García
Trombone: Pedro Deheza
Piano: Aurelio Galicia
Bass: David Pérez
Percussion: Hipólito González
Maracas: Paulino Rivero

BURUNDANGA

LEAD SINGER: EUGENIA LEÓN
COMBO: LA RUMBANTELA
CONDUCTOR: OSMANI PAREDES

Recording engineer: Luis Gil
Assistant to Annette Fradera: Renata Ramos

Recorded at Peerless's Pedro Infante studio and at El Cuarto de Máquinas
studio in Mexico City in Autumn 1995.

A production of Laura Esquivel under the direction of Annette Fradera

Musicomedia S.C./México
Fax (525) 513 40 17

Special thanks to CECUT (Tijuana)

Vocal fragment of Track 11 taken from "Versos de Pastorela" contained on
the LP *Tradiciones Musicales de la Laguna*, edited by the INAH.
(Excerpt from "Versos de Pastorela":
". . . Huélguense de ver al niño y acabado de nacer . . .")
Fieldwork, recording, and notes: Irene Vázquez Valle
Transfer, editing, and sound: Guillermo Pous
Postproduction and sound effects: Rogelio Villanueva

ABOUT THE ILLUSTRATOR

An award-winning illustrator, **Miguelanxo Prado** has collaborated in numerous animated film and television projects. He has a weekly comic strip, which is syndicated throughout Europe and Latin America, and he has published twelve books. Laura Esquivel saw his work in Mexico and asked him to collaborate with her on *The Law of Love*. Mr. Prado lives in Spain.

ABOUT THE JACKET ARTIST

Montserrat Pecanins was born in Barcelona and lives in New York and Mexico. Her theater boxes and miniature cabarets have been exhibited in Tiffany's windows and have adorned the Rockefeller Center skating rink at Christmas, as well as many other festive celebrations.

ABOUT THE AUTHOR

Originally published in 1990, *Like Water for Chocolate (Como agua para chocolate)* won **Laura Esquivel** international acclaim. The film based on the book, with a screenplay by Laura Esquivel, swept the Ariel Awards of the Mexican Academy of Motion Pictures, winning eleven in all, and went on to become the largest grossing foreign film ever released in the United States. In 1994 *Like Water for Chocolate* won the prestigious ABBY award, which is given annually by the American Booksellers Association to the book the members of the organization most enjoyed hand-selling. The book has been translated into thirty languages and there are over three million copies in print worldwide. Ms. Esquivel lives in Mexico.